About the Book

Filthy Beautiful Love

I never expected to watch Sophie walk away –
especially not with her virginity intact. She was mine. She
just didn't know it yet. New goal: Seal the deal and rock
her world so thoroughly she never wanted to leave again.

Highly sexual and emotionally charged, Filthy
Beautiful Love is the provocative conclusion to Filthy
Beautiful Lies.

Chapter One

Sophie

"Are you going to tell me where the money came from?" Becca looks at me expectantly over the rim of her third glass of Chardonnay.

"Colton," my liquor-loosened tongue reveals before I can filter it. "He and I had a kind of arrangement."

"How did you meet him?" Becca asks, her gaze inquisitive.

"Next question." I might be several drinks past drunk but there's no way I'm telling her about the auction. I needed to maintain *some* dignity in this shameful situation.

Her eyes never stray from mine as she takes another contemplative sip. We're sitting at a tiny bar in the lobby of our hotel. When I'd found out about Colton's marital status, I'd fled for home, broken hearted and destroyed. Becca convinced me we needed a girl's weekend away. I'd done one better and flew us to Rome on a whim. So here we sit, halfway around the world and all we can think to discuss is the exact topic that sent me running in the first place. *Awesome.* I take another healthy swig of my beverage. *God, don't they have anything stronger than wine in this country?*

"What kind of arrangement can you make with a man where he just gives you half a million dollars, Soph?" Her tone is accusatory. Good thing she doesn't know about the rest of the money, which is tucked inside my own bank account. I know my family has a lot of questions about where the money for Becca's treatment came from, and so far, I haven't said a word. Until now. Her eyes grow wide and she slaps a hand over her mouth. "Oh my God, were you like, his sex slave?" She giggles.

5

My cheeks burn brightly, but I shake my head. "You'd have to actually have sex for that to be the case, I'd think…"

She's still giggling, so I know she has no idea she's hit the nail on the head. *Ding, ding, ding. We have a winner.*

"Let's not talk about the money, Becca. It's not important. Colton was willing to provide it, and I don't regret anything because it helped you get better. Please just let it go," I plead with her to let it drop. Her health is cooperating for once and I want to enjoy this trip – just us. I don't want to even think about the name Colton Drake. It's much too painful.

"If he's as hot as you've said he is, I would have had a hard time not ripping his clothes off and jumping him. Oops, I'm sorry, my vagina accidentally landed on your penis."

I crack a smile at her change in topic. Of course it's about sex. Becca's not a virgin and she's much more forward about sex than I am. You'd think it'd be the opposite, but somehow, I'm the cautious one, whereas being sick from a young age taught her to grab life by the balls and live it to the fullest. I envy her in that.

Her first sexual experience was with a boy in the cancer treatment center. He was seventeen and she was just fifteen at the time. She'd told me every single detail, a proud gleam in her eye. It was inspiring how she let nothing stand in her way. I'd summoned her inner strength the night I stood on that auction block waiting to be sold.

"Soph?" she asks, drawing me back from my faraway thoughts. "Are you okay?"

"I miss him," I admit softly. "That's crazy, right?"

"Not crazy. That's normal when you break up with someone, from what I hear."

"I didn't break up with him. He wasn't my boyfriend. He's married, remember?" I'd told Becca nearly everything – about me living with him, us growing closer,

7

and about being naked in the pool when his wife arrived home one afternoon. Of course Colton tried to stop me, all but tackling me in the hallway of his mansion that suddenly felt cold and foreign to me. I waited for him to try and deny it, to explain it all to me, but sadly, it was all true. Stella was his wife. He'd been married the entire time.

"Technically. But I still think you need the rest of the story. Obviously his wife wasn't living there. How long have they been separated?"

I shrug. "He hasn't had sex in two years." Unless he was lying about that too. I don't know what to believe anymore.

"Damn, that's quite a dry spell. And if he's as hot as you've said he is…it's not like he didn't have offers, right?"

I was one of those offering. I blush, realizing I'd practically put my vagina on a silver platter for him and he repeatedly turned it down. It's enough to give a girl low self-esteem.

"Listen, it's okay to miss him. It's okay to feel confused." She reaches across the space between us and grabs my hand. Despite being six minutes younger than me, Becca has always been wise beyond her years. Her advice is thoughtful and spot on. She downs the last of her wine. "But we're in frickin Rome for a once in a lifetime girls trip, so there will be no moping allowed. We're going to have fun."

Yay, fun. My heart feels like it's been fed through a paper shredder. I nod and force a smile onto my face. Becca's right. This really could be a once in a lifetime trip for me and her. Who knows what the future holds. I can't waste time feeling sorry for myself. Of course that's easier said than done.

I miss Colton's bed, his scent, the feel of his rough stubble against my cheek when we kissed. I miss everything about him. Just as we'd started to grow close, everything I'd come to love was ripped away from me, leaving a gaping hole in my chest.

Forcing the thoughts of him from my mind, I throw back the rest of my wine and glance at the charming ambience of the bar around us, hoping this trip will be the distraction I need.

***

The next morning, the knock on our hotel room door surprises us both. Becca and I exchange a look. She shrugs while I move across the room to answer it. At least we're both dressed.

Once the door opens, I stumble back, looking up into dark, intense eyes framed in heavy lashes that I'd recognize anywhere.

"Colt..." I murmur, utterly shocked to see him here in Italy.

"Soph..." he returns, his voice gravelly.

"W-What are you doing here?" I'm breathless and I don't know why.

"You," he says simply, his eyes burning on mine.

Everything I've tried to forget slams into me at once. His deep blue eyes that are hungry and seeking. His masculine jawline, his height, and even his scent evoke a sense of deja-vu. I remember everything in perfect detail, including the wicked pleasure he gave my body. I suppress a warm shiver.

"Hi cupcake," Pace says, grinning at me from behind Colton.

What in the world? Remembering my manners, I reluctantly let my gaze wander from Colton to greet Pace and I introduce him to Becca. Utterly at a loss for what they're both doing here, I step aside to let them in.

Becca's wide smile as she shakes Pace's hand reminds me of the affect meeting him for the first time can have on a girl. Her cheeks are rosy and her eyes are alight with mischief. Oh, this isn't good.

"And this must be the infamous Colton Drake," she says, locking eyes with Colton next.

Watching my sister as she appraises Colton's perfect form from head to toe, my chest gets tight and I feel tears sting my eyes. Then my anger starts to rise, remembering his betrayal. But I'm in such a state of shock, that it takes me a moment to get my mouth working. "Ignore him. He's leaving," I say, remembering that he and I are through.

"Awe, don't be like that," Pace says. "We just spent ten hours flying coach to come see you. The least you can do is invite us in, and let me flirt with your sister." His lopsided smile is back and I swear, I practically see Becca's knees buckle.

"You flew coach for me?" I blurt without thinking.

"It was the only option. The jet wasn't available. I wanted the next flight out and first class was full," Colton explains.

I try to imagine these two men — who are each well over six-feet tall folded into cramped airplane seats for hours on end.

"Now that's love," Pace remarks under his breath.

"This is where you're staying?" Colton peers around the tiny room, which takes all of three seconds.

Splurging was coming on this trip in the first place — I wouldn't waste the precious money I had on first class airfare or a fancy hotel room. Even though Becca had responded well to the treatment so far, there was no guarantee that she'd stay healthy, or that she wouldn't need another round in a pricey treatment facility.

"What's wrong with the room? Not up to your high standards?" I remark, crossing my arms in front of my chest.

He frowns. "Let me upgrade you. Take you somewhere proper," Colton says, his dark eyes finding mine again.

How dare he? He can't waltz in here, interrupt my vacation and then insult where I'm staying. He doesn't control everything. The urge to push him from the room and slam the door in his face is nearly overwhelming. I pull a deep breath into my lungs, just as he reads my uneasy expression and takes a step back.

"Never mind. As long as you're comfortable." He eyes the bed linens like he's checking for bedbugs.

Asshole.

"I am." Or at least I was until he arrived out of the blue and completely threw my emotions into a tailspin.

Pace crosses the room, pulls out the small chair from the desk and plops down. His frame dwarfs everything in our tiny efficiency. He looks out of place, but in a good way. "I didn't realize you had a sister. Sexy obviously runs in the family." He throws a wink toward Becca.

"We're twins," Becca informs him.

We always looked a bit different, and now more than ever. With Becca's hair growing back in, it just reaches the tops of her shoulders and she wears it wavy and messy. My hair falls like a thick curtain down my back and is as straight as an arrow. She's also about fifteen pounds thinner than me. Chemo will do that to you.

"Mmm," Pace growls, his eyes wandering between us. "I've always had a secret twin fantasy." The hungry look in his eyes is enough to bring a woman to her knees. Becca stands zero chance against his charms.

Colton steps closer to my side, his fists tightening as he shoots an evil glare toward Pace. "Don't make me kill you as soon as we've landed. It would really dampen the trip."

"Don't make me confiscate your balls. Now go

talk to your woman," Pace challenges.

I open my mouth to correct him. I am no one's *woman*, but my brain flashes back to that fateful night when Colton purchased me from the auction. I accepted the money—and spent a good chunk of it. Does that mean I still belong to him despite finding out he's married?

I cursed the stupid contract, I cursed the man himself for holding my heart captive. That was never part of the plan.

When I meet his eyes again, he looks lost, broken, and it tugs at something deep inside me. As much anger as I felt discovering that he'd lied to me the entire time we were together, I still have feelings for him. I can't just turn them off. Despite his obvious shortcomings, he helped my sister, and he made me feel alive. He was everything I never knew I wanted.

"Can we go out into the hall and talk for a minute?" Colton asks, his voice whisper soft.

"Hear him out, kid. Do it for me," Pace says, dimples out in full force, like he knows they're impossible to refuse. *The jerk.*

I swallow and give an imperceptible nod before following him into the hall. He flew halfway around the world; the least I could do was listen to his explanation. Maybe it will give me some much needed closure. Maybe I can get the answers I need to move on and also figure out where we stand with respect to the large chunk of money exchanged between us. He never collected on his end of the bargain after all, I am still a virgin.

Once we're out in the hall, Colton stands before me, looking directly into my eyes. "So, that's Becca, huh?" He tips his head toward the door.

"Yeah."

"She looks good – healthy, I mean."

I nod. "Yeah, the treatment worked – so far. She goes in for another round in two weeks, but with

17

everything that's happened, it seemed like a good time to get away – for both of us." She and I have never done anything like this, but it was part of my plan to start actually living.

He nods. "I see."

We're silent for several seconds and Colton's hand twitches like he wants to touch me, but he doesn't. Thank God.

"And would your running away to another country have anything to do with…Stella?"

I flinch involuntarily. I hate that he's just said her name. It immediately conjures images of that day in the pool, when my whole little world shattered. In the country of Italy, her name should not exist.

"Will you tell me the story?" I ask.

"Anything you want to know."

"Are you getting divorced?"

"That's up for debate."'

"Then I'm leaving." I turn for the door, my hand gripping the knob.

"No. Stay. Please hear me out," Colton pleads, prying my fingers from the door handle.

His hand on my skin sends a flash of heat through me at the memory of what those hands can do. He's still the only man who's made me come. I shudder as though the memory singes some part of me.

I hear a wave of girly laughter behind the door. It warms me to hear Becca enjoying herself, and it grounds me in the moment. Turning to face Colton again, I draw a deep, calming breath. "Do you love her?"

"No." His voice is sure, steady. "I never loved her like I should have."

My shoulders relax just slightly. Even if my body wants to run, and my head is screaming at me to flee, my heart has grown attached to this man. And for better or worse, part of me needs to hear him out, to understand

19

this messy situation I've found myself in. Maybe if I can make sense of it, then I can move on.

"Please let me explain, that's all I'm asking." He raises his palms in a placating gesture.

I've never seen him look so devastated and broken. Dark circles line his eyes and he hasn't shaved in days. Even though I've agreed to hear him out, a wave of nausea washes through me. *Am I prepared to handle whatever he's about to tell me?* I fasten one hand against the wall for support. "I just need a minute…"

He releases a heavy exhale and I swear what looks like regret washes over his features. "I will give you all the time you need, sweetness," he whispers.

The nickname against his lips presses like a weight onto my chest. My heart feels heavy, thudding dully against my ribcage.

Another fit of Becca's giggles greet us from behind the door.

"He's probably trying to de-pants her," Colton says.

"I don't think she'd mind much."

"Should we check on our siblings while we're giving you a minute?"

I nod. We might as well. I don't think I'm ready to hear the entire sordid tale about how the man I was falling for is married and by the sounds of it, not necessarily planning to divorce. A stiff drink might help ease some of this ache in my chest too.

Back inside the cramped hotel room, Becca and Pace are standing near the open windows, deep in conversation. I've never seen her look so happy and chipper. She's openly flirting and preening like a peacock, twirling a lock of hair around her finger and smiling up at him brightly. Our vacation is about to get a lot more interesting.

Realizing we're back in the room, Becca turns to

me. "Soph, did you know Pace spent a semester studying here in Rome? He's going to take me sightseeing – show me all the best spots that aren't in those travel guides we bought."

So much for kicking Pace and Colton out. This was supposed to be a girl's trip, but I won't deny Becca anything, and I can tell she'd love to spend more time in Pace's company. It's that damn crooked grin and dimple of his that just beg you to come out and play.

"How did you know where I was?" I ask Colton.

"Kylie," he confirms.

I'd started working with Kylie at Colton's charity organization a few days a week and it didn't feel right to leave her hanging. And while I'd only intended to tell her that I would be out of town for a while, she somehow got me to spill the beans about my trip to Rome.

"When did you get here?" he asks.

"Last night." It's almost noon, but with the jetlag

and the wine we consumed last night, Becca and I haven't unpacked a thing. It's actually a small miracle we're up and showered.

"I assume you haven't had lunch yet. Let's get you something to eat and I'll explain everything." He turns to my sister who is for some reason squeezing Pace's bicep while he grins adoringly down at her. "Pace, Becca, how about a quick bite to eat before you start your sightseeing?"

"I'm game," Pace says.

"Me too," Becca chimes in, grabbing her purse.

I want to sulk and stomp my feet and refuse to go, but denying myself food seems like a childish way to punish him. "There's room service." I nod toward the menu sitting on top of the dresser.

"No way we're sitting inside the room all day, Soph," Becca encourages. "Come on, it's just lunch."

I shoot her a scowl. *Traitor.* I make a mental note

to not be so nice to her. Like saving her some hot water for her shower this morning–that was a one-time deal. She might think she's helping by interfering with me and Colt, but she's not.

I gather up my belongings, my purse, sunglasses and the Euros I changed over before we left the airport, and follow the group to the elevator. This should be interesting.

Chapter Two

Sophie

The sidewalk café is beautiful and understated. Black wrought iron tables and chairs with fluffy wine-colored cushions, and ivy growing along a little trellis that separates the street from the sidewalk café complete the space. It's sunny and clear with blue skies overhead, but not too warm, and I find it hard to hold onto my sour mood.

Colton suggests a white wine from a local vineyard and when it arrives, I've never tasted anything quite so light, crisp and refreshing. His impeccable taste is just one more thing that's easy to love about him. But I can't go there. Won't. My body has already betrayed me by springing to life when he's near, like when he helped me

25

into my chair and his hand brushed against my lower back. It left my skin tingling. And when he slid out the chair across from me, his tall, commanding presence caused a little flutter in my chest. I need to keep myself in check.

His eyes roam over my exposed skin–my bare shoulders peeking from the tank top–and my chest and neck flush with heat.

I'm glad our siblings are picking up the slack when it comes to making conversation, because Colton and I remain completely silent. Small talk doesn't seem to fit my mood and I'd have no idea what to say regardless. They chatter away without a care in the world while Colton and I exchange serious looks.

"So how long are you guys here?" Becca asks.

"Depends," Pace says.

"On?" I challenge. As far as I'm concerned, Colton has made his point, showing up here in some masculine display to claim his property. He can piss off now, thank you very much.

Colton's sad eyes slide over to mine. "I want a chance," he says, his voice dark.

A chance to explain, or a chance with me? I'm thankful for the large wraparound sunglasses that shield my eyes from his.

"Isn't that what she gave you all those weeks in LA?" Becca asks, coming to my rescue.

Thank you, God. The sane and feisty sister I know and love is back. I look over at Becca, communicating my gratitude without needing to speak.

Colton watches the interaction happening between me and Becca, no doubt wondering what I've told her about my time in Los Angeles. I hope he knows me well enough to know I'd never divulge our secret.

"I fucked up. It was wrong not to tell you…" Colton's voice is thick with emotion, unlike I've ever heard him before.

"Stella is a mega-beast who…" Pace starts.

Colton holds up one hand, silencing his brother. "No, Pace. This is my mess. I will fix it."

I have no idea why, but the sudden urge to ease his pain and anguish flares up inside me. "I'm here aren't I?" I say, meeting Colton's eyes. Of course, I'm not brave enough to remove the cover of my sunglasses, but still.

His sad look dissipates ever so slightly.

An hour later, we're on our second bottle of wine before the waitress even thinks to bring the lunch menu. I realize that Colton's suggestion of grabbing a *quick bite to eat* is quickly turning into an all afternoon affair. The pace of this country's meal times are nothing like the US.

"Let's order some lunch, shall we?" Pace, asks, handing me a menu printed entirely in Italian.

Our food is finally delivered, and while we eat Becca opens up about her treatment. I can't help but notice Colton leans forward on his elbows to absorb every word. He knows the hefty price tag for the treatment was made possible by his generous winning bid. And maybe it's the charitable side to him, but I can see in his reverent expression that something inside of him feels proud to have helped.

When Becca probes Colton about his work, he makes some offhand remark about investment banking and then launches into a detailed discussion about his charity foundation. They're close to fulfilling their mission in Africa. The new school he's built will have their grand opening soon.

Becca is in awe listening to him – clearly he's a great catch who just got even better in her eyes.

"Sophie's work is missed. She was a big help those weeks spent getting Kylie caught up." He reaches for my hand and I move it under the table.

Though the conversation buzzes around me, I can barely keep up. My head is filled with questions about

Colton's marriage to a woman he admittedly doesn't love. Why did he marry her? Where has she been while I've been sleeping in their bed? My entire relationship with him now feels tainted.

Despite our precarious start to things, I'd started to believe that he'd been brought into my life for a reason. Sent to me like a guardian angel to heal Becca and awaken me sexually. I'd spent two months living with him, growing close, falling for him.

I wonder now more than ever about why he never slept with me. Was it because he didn't want to be unfaithful to his wife?

"Sophie?" Colton's voice cuts through the one in my head. "More wine?"

I shake my head. "I'd rather just get going back to the hotel."

He checks his watch and frowns. "Okay. That should be all right."

We finish our lunch of insalata, warm bread, white wine and several bottles of sparkling water. After Colton pays for the meal, Pace and Becca rise from the table, looking slightly tipsy and eager to set off on their exploration.

Colton and I walk side by side in silence all the way back to the hotel. But there are so many new sights, sounds and smells to take in, that I hardly notice the stiff uncomfortable silence that's settled between us. Just navigating the uneven cobblestone streets in my strappy sandals takes extra concentration.

When we reach the hotel, Colt opens the door and ushers me through, his warm palm once again settling against my spine and leaving a rush of tingles in its wake.

A young man dressed in a hotel uniform stops us in the lobby.

"A new key for you, Miss." His Italian accent caresses the words, making them sound much sexier than they are.

"I have a key." I hold it up.

"Yes, but for your new suite. Floor seventeen." He folds the key card in my hand while simultaneously removing the old one.

I recall Colton stopping to talk in hushed voices with the concierge before we left the hotel. Is this his doing?

He raises an eyebrow and shrugs. "I just wanted you to be comfortable."

I bite my tongue to avoid pointing out that I'd been more comfortable before he appeared and started interfering, but deep down inside, I know he's just trying to be nice, as annoying as it might be. He can't win me back with thoughtful gestures and sweet remarks. Call me crazy, but I have a rule about dating man who are married: I don't.

"You shouldn't have," I bite out and turn for the

elevator, punching the button repeatedly with my thumb. I notice Colton waiting beside me and I give him a pointed stare. "I guess you can wait in the lobby for Becca and Pace's sightseeing date to end."

"You promised me we could talk," he says, his tone making clear his displeasure.

Yes, but that was before the wine and the possessive stares he treated me to all during lunch. I don't trust myself alone in a room with him right now. "I don't think being alone in a hotel room with a married man is proper."

He releases a low growl of frustration just as the elevator doors open and drags me inside.

Warning bells are going off inside my head. I'm about to be alone with a man who still holds power over my heart despite his unavailable relationship status.

Be strong, Sophie.

Colton

Pinning Sophie to the wall of the elevator, my hands clench into fists above her head. It's taking every ounce of self-control I have not to push my hips into hers and claim her mouth. I know I've lost the right, but my body refuses to understand that.

I can see her pulse thrumming in her neck as I bend down near her ear. "Don't push me right now. My emotions are all over the fucking place – something very new for me, I can assure you."

She shoves both hands against my chest, pushing me back several paces. "Oh, *your* emotions are all over the place? Try putting yourself in my shoes." Her voice rises frantically. "I was buck-naked in your goddamn pool trying to seduce you when your *wife* showed up." The word wife is spat from her mouth like a sour bomb.

"You ran out on me before I had the chance to explain. You wouldn't answer my calls and now I've flown six thousand miles just to set the record straight with you." I take a deep breath and straighten my posture. Arguing with her won't get me anywhere. Of course she has a right to be mad. "Listen, Soph. I needed to see you. I'm coming upstairs to talk to you."

After an intense standoff her gaze falls to the floor as she realizes further negotiation will be pointless. "What floor am I on?"

"Top floor," I answer. The best suite they have. Obviously.

Realizing we're just standing in the stationary elevator that hasn't yet moved from the ground level, she gingerly reaches out and presses the button. My mouth lifts up in a smile. *Progress.*

Per my instructions, Sophie and Becca's luggage

has been moved into the suite. There's a moderately sized living room, two separate bedrooms, each with its own washroom and a tiny balcony overlooking the courtyard fountain. She takes a minute to navigate the rooms, lightly running her fingers along a gilded antique credenza and bending at the waist to smell the fresh arrangement of white blossoms on the coffee table.

I take every second I can to just drink her in. Even though it's only been three days since I've seen her, held her in my arms, slept with her warm body next to me, it feels like much longer. The privilege to touch her has been ripped away, and my body riots in silent agony, my heart aching and my fists clenching uselessly at my sides. *I fucking hate this.*

We need to talk like civilized adults, but fuck if I know how to start.

"Soph..." I begin.

"Colt..." She says at the same time.

We share an awkward smile.

"Come sit down." I gesture to the sofa – neutral territory and she obeys, slipping off her sandals and curling her legs underneath her as she sinks into the cushion farthest away from me.

"Ask me anything you want to know. No more secrets," I promise.

Bouncing one knee up and down, she twists the ring on her thumb. "How long have you been married?"

I release a heavy sigh and push my fingers into my hair. Much longer than I want to admit.

"If you try to hide things…if you're going to be evasive…" She swallows.

"Anything you want to know. Even if the truth is hard to hear," I confirm. As much as I'd like to protect her from the ugly truth, I won't. Not if that's not what she wants. "I've been married for four years. For the past two we haven't lived in the same state."

"Why was she at your house that day?"

"Who the fuck knows with her. We've been trying to settle our divorce for a long time. But neither of us can seem to agree on anything."

She licks her lips, thinking over this information. "Is she the reason you went to New York?"

"Yes, Stella lives in New York with her boyfriend. I went there to try and talk to her about the terms of our divorce in person. That didn't work."

Her forehead creases. "She has a boyfriend?"

I nod. "Our former gardener. I found out they started fucking after we got married."

Her mouth tugs down in a frown. "Oh."

"It turns out that she never loved me, and even though my family warned me about her motives, I couldn't see it. I wanted a woman in my life, and I don't know..." I rub my temples absently. "Maybe it had to do with losing my mother at such a young age... But I liked the company,

38

the companionship of someone by my side. Someone warm and loving to share my life with." I sound like a complete pussy, but that was how the twenty-four year old me saw the world.

And Stella was the perfect trophy wife, accompanying me to work functions, dressing in the latest fashions and always a happy smile on her lips. Too bad it had all been fake.

"What happened?" Sophie asks, her tone softening.

"Things changed as soon as we got engaged. I thought it was just stress over planning the wedding–she wanted it to be the affair of the decade, something the Los Angeles elite would be buzzing about for years to come– she put way too much pressure on herself planning it. I didn't see at the time that it was all for show. It was more about the dress and the party and French champagne than it was about me and her."

Sophie chews on her lip, listening intently. I have no fucking clue why I'm unloading all this…but something tells me if I have any hope at salvaging things between us, I need to bare my soul.

I clear my throat and continue. "And even though my brothers tried to talk me out of it, I had convinced myself that it was all going to be fine. I wasn't going to call off my wedding simply because my fiancé was turning into a bridezilla. I figured it would all settle down after the wedding day."

"But it didn't?" Sophie asks softly.

"No. She was distant, and cold. Not at all like the smiling, charming girl I fell for in the first place. Once the rock was on her finger and the ink on the marriage license was dry, she turned into a completely different person. The one I suspected she'd actually been all along. She'd played me. Married me for my money and I'd fallen for it like a lovesick fool."

"I'm sorry, Colt..." she starts.

"No, don't." She shouldn't be the one apologizing to me. The headache I'd felt coming on earlier was full-on throbbing in my temples. I continued, "After the game Stella pulled on me, it made it hard to even think about trusting another woman. Being separated for the past two years, I tried dating causally. I didn't want to, but my brothers occasionally set me up with a woman. Behind every sweet smile and every flirty look was someone only interested in my bank roll and the lifestyle I could provide. I wanted a genuine connection, not a trophy wife. But I realized with my status and my wealth, real love wasn't going to be something easy to find."

"Then why go to that auction?" Her confusion is etched between her eyebrows as she waits for me to answer.

"To put it bluntly?" I smirk.

She nods for me to go ahead.

41

"A man has his limits. The pent up sexual frustration of being celibate for two years…I was horny as fuck and needed to get laid."

Her mouth twitches in a smile.

"That's the complete truth. I knew exactly what I was paying for and that there'd be no chance of feelings or false promises."

"Why not just hire an escort?"

I shrug. The thought had crossed my mind a few times. "I guess I'm not the kind of guy to hire an escort. I wanted something more discreet. I couldn't have that information getting leaked. CEOs who get caught hiring prostitutes usually end up on the evening news."

She nodded in silent understanding.

"With the auction, I liked the medical testing, non-disclosure agreements and confidentiality promised to me. Plus the companionship angle we covered before."

"But you never…we never…" She pauses.

"I never fucked you," I finish for her.

She lifts her chin in indignation. "Why not? Is it because you would have felt like you were cheating on her?" she asks, her big blue eyes locked onto mine.

I reach for her hand, pulling it into my lap, unable to resist the physical warmth it provides. "No. It's because I would have felt like I was cheating on you. You deserved more and I knew it."

Her bottom lip trembles and the urge to suck it into my mouth flares up inside me.

Pulling her hand away, Sophie rises to her feet. "You can't say things like that." There's anger in her eyes and I'm left speechless. I can't even begin to imagine all the thoughts and emotions running through her head. So I won't try. She moves to the window and looks out solemnly.

Rising to my feet, I stand behind her, resisting the urge to pull her close. "I can't lose you," I whisper. "Not when I feel like my life is finally falling into place. You were the missing piece. You were the cheese to my macaroni." I smile lightly, hoping she remembers.

She turns to face me. Her soft gaze is pinned on mine and I can tell we're both remembering the time we spent together. It just felt right. "I can't do this, Colton. I was developing real feelings for you."

Was? I *know* I'm falling for her, terrifying as it fucking is. I shake the thought away, once again trying to convince myself that my interest in her is only about seeing the arrangement through.

"You're married," she reminds me.

Tramping down my emotions, I swallow. "Only legally. And if I can just get her to agree to the terms, I'll sign off on the divorce…"

"Wait. You're the one holding up the divorce?" Anger flashes in Sophie's normally calm blue eyes. The change in her is unmistakable. It's like I've inadvertently tripped some wire and a bomb is about to detonate. I take

a hesitant step back.

"Yes."

"But…I don't understand…"

Fuck. How do I explain this without further

upsetting her?

"If I divorce her, she wins. She'll take half of

everything, plus I'll be ordered to pay her spousal

support." It's not about the money – well, I guess it is,

because splitting up my millions will put my investment

into the Africa project at risk. It means I'll have fallen for

her game, hook, line and sinker. Stella one, Colt zero. But

worse than that, the funding for the school, hospital and

all the projects I had planned would be stopped dead in

their tracks as my money is tied up in a legal battle. I won't

let my personal fuckup be the cause of so much

destruction. I'm funneling every bit of money I have into

this charity and I won't sacrifice a single dollar to keep

Stella in Manolo Blahniks while children go hungry. *Fuck no.*

"You..." Her eyes widen and then slam closed. "You didn't have a pre-nup, and now your male pride is too damn stubborn to take the hit financially." She blinks up at me and something twists deep inside my gut.

She's right about the pre-nup, I was a fucking fool. Twenty-four years old when we tied the knot and thought I was in love. But she's wrong about the rest. "This has nothing to do with male pride. My goal all along has been to wait her out, and complete my project in Africa before finalizing the divorce. I won't have my money tied up in some court battle while I could be doing something actually fucking useful with it."

Sophie's judging stare and her rigid posture force me to see that maybe this isn't all going to end well. After surviving Stella, I need a woman who understands my drive and desire to see some good in the world. I thought

Sophie would be that woman. But perhaps I was wrong. I take a calming breath and struggle to clear my head.

Sophie moves across the room, her posture stiff as she goes to the far window that looks onto the courtyard below. I cross the room in a few long strides and stand behind her, breathing in the scent of her hair. "Soph…" I murmur.

Her shoulders relax and she sniffs like she's crying.

Spinning her to face me, I see that her face is red and a single tear tumbles along her porcelain cheek.

"Don't cry." I brush the dampness away with my thumb. "You're all I want. The rest, Stella, the paperwork, I'll figure it out. I just need time. And I need your faith in me." I don't know why that's suddenly so important, but it is. Her eyes drift closed and she doesn't protest. It's a start.

I've never groveled like this before, but I've also never felt quite as strongly about a woman as I do about

Sophie. Unable to resist the urge to touch her, I run my fingertips along her exposed arms, lightly caressing her smooth skin.

Sophie swallows and blinks up at me. Leaning down to lower my mouth to hers, I whisper against her lips. "You're mine, sweetness."

My cock was half hard all through lunch, but now that we're alone, the beast is demanding attention. I've traveled thousands of miles to get her to listen, and now the last thing I want to do is talk. I'm craving her like a drug.

Her mouth parts and I take the opportunity to gently kiss her full bottom lip, and then the top, carefully peppering her sweet mouth with tender kisses.

Her hands fist in my shirt and for just a moment I think she's going to push me away, but she tugs me closer and my kisses go from chaste to hot in two seconds flat. The knowledge that I haven't lost her sends a thrill racing through me.

My tongue pushes past her parted lips and caresses hers. Goddamn, I've missed the things this mouth can do. The raging erection in my pants remembers all too well.

The need to taste her, to consume every part of her flares within me. And knowing that there's a bed in the next room sends my mind spinning with possibilities. I want more. I want it all, everything she has to offer, but I force myself to slow and meet her eyes, checking for any sign of displeasure. Her look is pure wanton lust.

My hand slips under the hem of the skirt she's wearing. If she knew my dark thoughts right now, she wouldn't have worn this in my presence. But she seems blissfully unaware that I want to fuck her hard and fast until she's sore and bowlegged from my cock repeatedly impaling her.

The man she's come to know exercises restraint

and control at every turn, but that man is nowhere to be found. Unable to hold back from touching her, I slide my hand up the outside of her thigh and feel her tremble, but she doesn't pull away. She doesn't move a single muscle.

Curving my hand around, I palm one rounded ass cheek that's soft and warm in my hand and knead the succulent flesh. She drives me fucking crazy with desire. I want her ass. I want every part of her.

Feeling bold, I slip one finger under the elastic of her panties and feel her draw a shuddering breath. *That's right baby. Let me touch you.*

"You want this, don't you?" I whisper against her collarbone.

She shakes her head.

"Don't lie to me, sweetness."

I caress a finger along her silken folds. She's already damp with desire. I drag my finger up her slit, parting her lips and find her clit. Using the pad of my index finger, I circle the little bundle of nerves and feel it swell. *Hell yeah*. Remembering the first time I got her off, my cock engorges with blood until it's rock hard and almost painful.

Sophie's hands ball into fists at her sides, and she looks like she's struggling with something. Her brow is knotted and her breathing is erratic, but she's not moving away, in fact she's leaning in to my touch, tilting her hips so I can rub her clit at just the right angle. I realize she's having some internal battle with herself. Her body wants this, but her head is telling her no. And my guess is that her hands are clenched tight to stop herself from reaching out and touching me. Surely she can feel my raging erection pressing into her hip.

It's okay, you can touch him, baby.

Please fucking touch him.

I want to feel her little fist curl around my shaft and squeeze. I feel like I'm going to die if she doesn't touch me soon. I'm two seconds away from pulling my cock out myself and stroking it until I come.

Just as Sophie begins to whimper softly and I can tell she's building toward release, she takes a step back just out of reach so that my hand slides from her panties. Her eyes are hungry and swimming with unspoken emotion.

Shit.

Chapter Three

Sophie

Colton's gaze skims over my features, like he's checking to be sure I'm okay before settling on my eyes again. Nothing about this is okay, but I'm powerless to stop it. I'm scared of feeling too much for him, and I'm scared of letting him go, so I do the only thing I can – I turn myself over to the visceral pleasure coursing through me, begging for a sweet release. My body is practically vibrating with need, but I need a moment to process what's happening, so I take a step back.

"Don't run away from this," he purrs.

Stalking closer, Colt anchors his hands to my waist, his long fingers biting into my hips as he lifts me up. My legs close around his waist, my core seeking friction against the hard ridge in the front of his pants.

I gasp at the crazy mix of emotions and raw sensation overtaking my system. I know I should stop him, push him away, I just don't want to. I miss this side of him. Suddenly I want to be on my knees before him with his hot, heavy cock in my mouth. Memories of our weeks spent together flood my senses, making it impossible to turn away.

"Colt…" I whisper. I have no idea what I'm asking for and his soft eyes plead with mine.

He supports my weight effortlessly with both hands resting under my butt. I want his fingers again…I was so close. And now I'm keyed up and confused.

"I'm tangled up in you. I can't let you go," he says, placing one more kiss against my mouth. He stares back at me for a moment. I can't take the broken quality to his voice, the way his warm palm slides against my exposed hip bone. Even though I shouldn't, I crave his touch. I've missed him. I've missed this. This growing connection between us. It takes every ounce of strength I have not to give in to him.

Before everything went to hell the afternoon his wife showed up, I felt like we were building toward something real – if not love, then something close. I wasn't experienced, but given the chance, I knew I could fall in love with Colton Drake. Which meant letting him into my hotel room, letting him kiss me and gaze into my eyes and break down all my walls was a dangerous move. My heart was on the line. But he'd tracked me down and chased me halfway around the world. That has to mean something, right?

"Sweetness," he murmurs in the husky tone that I've come to recognize means he's aroused.

My voice disappears as any words of protest die in my throat. I have to tell him no. I need to make him leave. He's done something that can't be undone. He led me to believe he was unattached and concealed the truth from me for weeks. I now wonder if he would have ever told me if Stella hadn't shown up. Despite my suspicions, I'd ignored my womanly instincts and turned myself over to him completely. I'd been ready to give him my virginity.

His fingertips edging under my skirt pull me from my thoughts. My core heats with the knowledge that his skilled fingers are just inches from where I want them. *Yes, yes yes.* My panties are soaking wet and I rock against him, but my raspy voice breaks the silence and contradicts everything my body is screaming for. "No…I can't…" I untangle my legs from his waist and drop to the floor.

"You want this just as badly as I do," he says, his voice deep and sure.

My eyes lift to his and apparently they tell him everything he needs to know. My desire for him is written all over my face. My thoughts betray me. And Colton takes full advantage, leaning in to kiss me again.

"Tell me there's still a chance," he whispers against my lips.

I swallow, but am unable to respond. I don't trust myself to say the right thing. I debate with myself, wondering if I could ever trust him again, if I could even fit into his lifestyle…

A bubble of feminine laughter and the sound of the door clicking open snap me back to my senses.

Becca and Pace waltz into the room carrying a half dozen shopping bags between them.

My sanity returns and I force a serious tone as I turn toward Colton. "It's time for you guys to go."

Goodbyes are exchanged between Pace and Becca while I avoid meeting Colton's dark eyes. I know if I do, I'll lose my resolve completely. I'm still reeling from that kiss, my body overheated and blood pumping wildly.

He pins me with a heated stare, leaning close enough that I can smell his cologne. The effect is dizzying.

"This isn't over. Have your fun with Becca and we'll talk when you get home."

I wish I could tell him he's wrong, that we are over, but I find myself unable to respond. He's giving me the space I need right now, but I have no idea what comes next.

Once they're gone, I grab a bottle of water from the stocked minibar and take a long swig, needing to cool myself down before turning to Becca. She doesn't say anything about the change in hotel room, but I see her eyes wandering around the space. "So what happened with Pace? I didn't think you guys would be back so quickly. In fact, I wondered if I'd see you again this entire trip. I figured you'd take one look at those dimples and you'd steal him away into a private hotel room." I grin at her in an attempt to lighten the tense mood.

"Trust me, it was tempting. He's gorgeous. And his tight little butt?" She fans herself dramatically.

"Seriously, those two are a lethal combination on the libido."

"There's a third one too. Their older brother Collins is every bit as lickable."

"Damn. Good genetics, I guess." She dumps the shopping bags out onto the sofa for me to inspect her goods. "After lunch, I actually started to worry about leaving you alone with Colt. I figured that wasn't the smartest idea, so we cut our outing short. We just walked around this cute little piazza and I went into a couple of boutiques." She holds a tiny sundress up to my frame. "I thought this would look cute on you."

"It's pretty." Lavender and touches of blue thread run through the soft fabric. "I can wear it with my strappy silver sandals."

"Exactly what I was thinking." She plucks a red mini skirt from the pile of clothes for herself. "Come on, get changed. We're going out."

Becca and I spent the rest of the day sightseeing and are currently seated at a quaint little bar, munching on olives and cheese and sipping delicious wine. I still can't believe Colton and Pace had actually flown to Italy in search of me. And as I sit here, slightly buzzed, I'm replaying our brief intimate encounter in my head.

"I know how you could get rid of it," Becca says, thoughtfully swirling the wine in her glass.

"What?"

"Your virginity. I mean, if you still want to, that is."

"How?" I ask, my mind spinning.

She tips her chin to a group of three cute Italian guys sitting together across the bar. "We could go pick up some hotties."

I briefly consider this. *When in Rome…Why the hell not?*

Because I still belong to Colton, that's why.

Even if I don't want to, some strange part of me knows it's true. He should be the one to take my virginity. When I think about his dark, hungry eyes that burn me up, his full mouth kissing my neck, and his thick, long cock, I know it has to be him. My chest flushes with heat and I'm transported right back to the moment earlier when I was right there – right on the edge –just a few more strokes of his fingers and I would have come apart. I always thought I needed a sex toy to get off, it turns out I just needed Colton.

"You're thinking about him again." Becca smirks at me.

"I shouldn't be."

"But you are."

***

The remainder of our trip is nearly perfect. Gorgeous summer weather, long afternoons spent wandering the beautiful and seductive city of Rome with my best friend by my side. But my nights are plagued with memories of Colton, though I suppose that's unavoidable given the situation.

After the first day when he and his brother Pace showed up here unexpectedly, I've heard nothing more from him. I'm grateful that I opted not to upgrade my cell phone service to include international calling. I know I wouldn't be strong enough to continue ignoring him if that were the case. As it is, every morning after breakfast, I have to force myself to walk past the hotel's one computer in the business center to avoid connecting to my email. The thought that there could be a note from Colton waiting for me weighs heavily on my mind.

As much as I try to convince myself that things are done between us, some part deep inside of me knows that's not true.

Chapter Four

Colton

Back in California, I throw myself into my work. It's the only way to keep my thoughts from drifting to Sophie. I'm brutal in meetings, coarse in my communications and tense all the fucking time. My emotions are all over the damn place and my need for sex has only quadrupled since being near Sophie again. My feelings of longing are only intensified wandering my big, empty house alone at night.

I've tried texting her a couple of times, but I've gotten no response. She returned from Rome last weekend and has been in touch with Kylie, which is the only reason I know anything.

I should feel relieved. Sophie knows the truth

now. Everything is out in the open. There's no more hiding my broken marriage from her and no one would ever need to know my dark secret about purchasing a sex slave. This whole thing could be over – we're free from our arrangement. Only I don't want to be.

I should just walk away, but I won't. I still want to fuck her. Shit, it goes deeper than that if I'm being honest with myself. I like her. Her genuine nature, her selflessness for putting herself up for auction. She's not like other girls. She made me macaroni for fuck's sake, and refused my help for additional money. She's not like the women in my past. Or she's damn good at faking it.

Either way, I want to make her mine. I tell myself it's just because I never got to have her. Weeks spent waiting while the sexual tension and anticipation between us built to epic proportions have left me with the world's most critical case of blue balls. Terror alert level red. My sac is about to combust. Shit, at this point, I wonder if I even remember how to fuck. It can't be that difficult, right? I shake away the sullen thoughts swirling in my brain.

I want to claim her body, to be the first man to penetrate her pussy. And as much as I try to deny it, something inside me wants more than that too. But the entire point of this whole charade was because I promised myself I wouldn't get entangled with a woman ever again. So much for that not happening. I'm in deep with Sophie. Completely wrapped up in a woman I may have zero chance of having. But I'm not backing down now. No fucking way.

I'd bought and paid for her virginity, something I was not inclined to let simply slip through my fingers due to some technicality.

When I think back to her hotel room in Italy, the way she let me touch her…before completely shutting down on me, my stomach twists into a knot.

I'm not used to being turned down, and it's not a feeling I want to grow accustomed to. I didn't get where I am today by lying dormant. Deciding to take matters into my own hands, I call Sophie once more, giving her one last chance before I show up on her parent's doorstep and drag her back to me.

I may have trust issues, and I still need to deal with Stella, but none of that is going to stop me from taking what's mine. And Sophie is mine.

Expecting her voicemail, like every other time I've called, I'm surprised when she answers on the fourth ring.

"Sophie?" The surprise is evident in my voice.

"Hi," she says casually.

"We need to talk." She's silent for several long moments, only the soft sounds of her breathing tell me she's still on the line.

"About what?" she asks finally.

"I have a new proposition for you."

66

When the limousine I've sent drops Sophie off in my driveway, looking bewildered and tired, I'm thankful that her parents live a few hours north of Los Angeles. It means I should be able to keep her here at least through the night. She will have to hear me out.

Stepping out into the sunlight, I greet her beside the car. My fists clench uselessly at my sides as the realization that she's not mine to take into my arms slams against me. I lift her bag from the brick walkway and force a smile onto my lips. "Thank you for coming."

She nods. "Thank you for sending the limo. That really wasn't necessary." She twists the ring on her thumb, obviously curious about why I've summoned her here when things seem like they're over between us.

"Let's go inside."

I let her walk ahead, appreciating the way her round little behind sways enticingly. I follow like a puppy on a leash.

Once inside, Sophie is all tentative steps and unsure glances. Deciding it'll be best to cut to the chase about why I've brought her here, I lead her into the den. The same room where I brought her that first night. Memories of her on her knees before me, taking my thick cock into her mouth and sucking me off with such skill and enthusiasm causes my dick to harden instantly. *Fuck*.

I take a breath and clear my throat, hoping that her eyes don't wander to the front of my trousers. "Have a seat."

Sophie complies, sitting carefully at the edge of the sofa. I wonder if the memories of that first night are burned into her brain as thoroughly as they are into mine. Despite my efforts, I'm unable to get the visual of her full pink mouth wrapped around the head of my cock out of my mind. The way her tongue teased down the length of my shaft and her hand curled around my base, stroking as she sucked me deep into her throat.

My needy erection zaps all my concentration and it takes me a moment to realize Sophie is speaking.

"Colton?" she blinks up at me, drawing me from the x-rated show currently playing in my head.

"I'm glad you came," I say.

She chews on her lower lip, almost as nervous as the first time I brought her home. Her gaze sweeps around the room and her spine is as straight as an arrow. She doesn't want to let her guard down and I assume it's because she doesn't trust herself with me. Good to know. I don't trust myself either.

"Can I get you anything? Wine? A bottle of water?"

She shakes her head. "What did you want to discuss? You were kind of vague on the phone."

She's right. I was vague —mainly because I had no idea what I could say to persuade her. I knew I needed to see her eyes – to read her expression in order to craft my proposal. And the nervous, unsure girl I see sitting before me means I need to proceed with caution. I'd considered pushing her, convincing her how good we are together physically and persuading her to be with me the way I know she wants. But now I see that I need to employ a different method, because watching her walk out that door again is not an option.

"I know I fucked up by keeping my marriage from you. In my eyes, it's over, and has been for years. The only thing missing is a couple of signatures on a piece of paper. But still, I see now how that hurt you. It was a dick move." She nods, meeting my eyes. I lick my lips and continue. "But I don't think that my past means all this has to come to an end."

"What are you proposing?" she asks, her voice is

tentative and slightly breathless.

I want to fuck you. To dominate your days and nights, and occupy your every waking thought – just like you occupy mine. "I want you to stay."

Her brows pinch together as she quietly watches me. She's not flat out rejecting the idea –it's a start.

Sophie

I watch Colton sitting across from me, his tall frame neatly folded into the arm chair. His breathing remains deep and steady while my own heart thumps like a hammer, causing my chest to heave.

The truth is I have no idea what I'm doing here, why I've agreed to come. If I'm honest it's because this man has some magnetic pull over me. I'm totally and completely unable to give him up, despite my intentions to stay away. And for some strange reason, I feel the slightest bit guilty that I'd walked out on our agreement before fulfilling my obligation. He never got what he paid for and that little detail is something I cannot easily forget.

He pulls a fortifying breath into his lungs and leans in slightly toward me. I know if he pulled me into his arms and kissed me, I'd be unable to resist and I find my gaze fluttering between his lips and his eyes as I wait for him to speak.

Finally, he does.

"I recall you saying that you liked having something of your own – living away from home and being independent for the first time," Colton says.

I remember the conversation well. It was one of the first times we sat down to a dinner prepared by his chef in the quiet dining room. I spoke too freely, bared too much of myself. But something in me likes that he remembers it with such detail. Not that I'm surprised, Colton exercises such authority over every facet of his life, of course he remembers.

"And I think you know that I liked having you here," he admits.

I nod in silent acknowledgement. *What is he saying?* We can't possibly continue dating, if that's even what we were doing. He's married. And he lied to me about it. Can

I even trust him?

"And I know Kylie would love for you to come back to work with her."

"Colton?" I ask, finally, my brows pinching together.

"There's no reason we can't remain friends."

"Friends?" My voice comes out too high as the shock of his suggestion whips through me.

His dark eyes roam over my face and he gives a slight nod, his mouth only hinting at a smile.

I have no idea what game he's playing at, but friends? Is that even possible for two people so attracted to each other?

As if reading my thoughts, Colton continues. "There's no reason this needs to come to an end, Sophie. I enjoy your company, and I think you feel the same. You can continue living here, we can take things between us slowly while I sort out my past and see where this goes."

"And our arrangement?" I ask.

His impish grin lights up his entire face. "Friends, as in no sex. Our agreement is off."

My belly twists as I realize I am no longer a hired sex slave, and an unwelcome sense of disappointment startles me. "I'm returning the money then."

"The money is yours. I never wanted to pay for sex, Sophie. I just didn't want that asshole bidding on you at the auction to go home with you. You were too good, too pure and beautiful to belong to him." His admission takes my breath away. I feel helpless and out of control and I want to cry.

"I've spent a good chunk of the money on Becca's treatment, and I have no way to repay you, but the rest I could return to you," I stammer.

"First off, I would never accept repayment. Had I known Becca before all this started, I would have gladly paid to enroll her in the experimental treatment program. And I'd never expect you to return the money."

"I don't feel right keeping the remainder of the money."

"It's yours to do with what you wish."

This conversation is like a game of ping-pong and my brain feels fuzzy. "So how would this work?" I ask, shocked to see I'm actually considering it.

"You agreed to give me six months," he reminds me.

"I also agreed to give you my virginity," I add.

"But I didn't take that."

"No, you didn't," I agree. A fact that I'm painfully aware of.

"Are you still intact?" he asks, his tone raspy and deep.

A warm current zips through me, flushing my cheeks and soaking my panties. "Of c-course." My voice is hoarse and Colton's dark eyes roaming on mine make it impossible to speak clearly.

I see the vein throb at the base of his throat. "Good girl," he admonishes.

I'd waited twenty-one years, did he really think I'd just thrown it away with some random guy in the two weeks we'd been apart? Why do I sense this is all some carefully crafted ploy to keep me here in his bed? "Where will I sleep?" I ask.

His mouth turns down just a fraction. "Wherever you like."

"A guest room I suppose," I say more to myself than to him as I think of his strange proposition.

"If you prefer."

He's being so amiable, so accommodating. The change is refreshing after the emotional hell he's put me through. I'm still unsure about what exactly he's proposing and if he really expects me to remain living here for the next six months, but for some strange reason, I don't hate the idea. We watch each other in silence for several moments, each of us digesting what it would mean for us to be just friends. My heart hurts just thinking about it. It would mean I couldn't touch him, I wouldn't feel the heat of his body pressing adamantly against mine. I release a little sigh. "If you're set on me keeping the money, I assume I'm free to spend it however I wish?"

"Of course you can," he says.

"Then I'd like to donate it to your charity work in Africa."

A slow smile uncurls on his lips. "Okay then."

***

I'd only come to Los Angeles to gather my belongings from the mansion and get closure from Colton by listening to whatever it was that he wanted to tell me. Instead, I find myself moving my clothing from his master closet into a guest room down the hall that smells of lint and furniture polish.

The bed is dressed in shell blue linens and the furniture is modern, clean lines in white enamel. A large mirror hangs on the wall and decorative sconces flank either side of the cream upholstered headboard.

I pull open the white gauzy drapes shading the large picture windows and look out at the pool below. A cool shudder passes through me and I wrap my arms around my middle. I have no desire to be anywhere near that pool and I snap the curtains closed, blocking it from view. Just seeing the crystal blue water sparkle in the sunlight brings on a fresh wave of pain and humiliation at the memory of Stella's cold glare and icy tone as she informed me, in no uncertain terms, that she was his wife. The word *wife* –in relation to Colton– doesn't resonate. Especially coming from that woman's mouth. I could never see him with someone like her. They just don't fit. It makes me wonder if I even know him at all. An even better reason to remain friends while I figure that out. I want more with Colton. I want back that raw feeling of sexual energy that flows so easily between us whenever he's near –but I will settle for friends – for now, as we navigate this bumpy road we'd found ourselves on.

After I've finished moving my meager belongings into my new room, I'm left feeling bored and alone. But rather than going to find Colton in this monstrous house, I flop down on the bed and dial Becca on my cell.

"Hey hey," she answers, chipper as ever, as though she hasn't battled aggressive stage-four cancer for the past several years.

"Hi." Her strength and determination to live take my breath away and suddenly complaining to her about my dilemma with Colton seems childish and immature.

"What's wrong?" she asks.

"Nothing," the lie slips easily from my mouth. "I just might be staying here longer than I expected."

"Oh? Did Mr. Sexy, Rich and Handsome win you back already?"

"Sort of," I admit. Colton had been more open and exposed than I had expected, and it tugged at something inside me. "He proposed that I continue living here and working with Kylie."

"And I take it you accepted?" she asks.

"I'm gonna try it," I confirm.

"I don't blame you. I wouldn't live with Mom and Dad either if I didn't have to."

We don't discuss the fact that she isn't able to live on her own for health reasons. It hurts to even think about.

"And what about you guys?" she asks. "Are you a couple again, or what?"

"No." This time my voice is firm. "He said just as friends and I agreed. We're going to take things slow while he works on his past."

"I think that's a good idea. I know you were happy there. But what made you reconsider? He's hung like a baby elephant, isn't he?"

"Becca!" I chastise her. "Always with the sex on the brain."

"I can't help it. It's better to let my mind drift there than to something more morbid. Penis is my happy place."

I can hear her smile through the phone and I like it. "Penis is a good thing."

"So…what are you going to do about Colton's peen?"

"Take it slow, just like he proposed. I'm pretty sure that means there's no peen in my future."

"Boo. You're boring. I'm going to go to McGilroy's and get a hot fudge sundae."

"Appetite's back?" I ask.

"Yup. I'll be fat before you know it."

Yeah right. The idea of Becca anything other than stick-skinny would be a miracle. She has a hard time keeping food down and thus trouble with her weight. "Have fun. Love you."

"Love you too, but you're the one who needs to have fun. Figure out a way to speed up his divorce so you can jump that boy."

"On it." I smile, and end the call.

I cradle the phone in my hands for several minutes after we end the call. God, I love my sister. After organizing my room the best I can, I decide to go off in search of Colton.

I find him sitting on a stool at the kitchen island, his tablet in front of him with an inbox full of emails that he's clicking his way through.

"Am I interrupting?" I ask, grabbing a bottle of water from the fridge.

"Of course not. Are you okay?"

I nod. "I just called Becca to tell her I'm staying."

He's quiet, but his calm demeanor tells me this makes him happy.

Rather than sitting at the stool next to him, I round the kitchen island and stand across from him, leaning my elbows against the slab of granite.

He chuckles at me. "What's on your mind, sweetness?"

I didn't realize I was that obvious. I straighten my shoulders and relax the line crinkling my brow. "You and Stella..." I shouldn't ask, I'm only torturing myself, but I can't help it. I need to know, because I just can't picture him with her. "I want to know the nature of your relationship. Was it like a regular marriage, with all the perks and benefits of marriage?"

He presses a button darkening the screen on his tablet and draws a steading breath. "What are you asking?"

"You lived here with her. I'm assuming this house is full of memories for you, and it's just strange for me to think of you with another woman living here, sleeping together in the bed I shared with you…"

"What do you want to know?" Colton asks.

"I guess what I want to know is…were you happy? Stella, in my very brief interaction, seemed quite different from me." She was all hardened exterior, sharp edges and manicured to the last inch of her.

"You were different. Fuck, you *are* different, Sophie."

I like knowing that perhaps what he and I shared was different from what he had with her. "How so?"

"You're soft and sweet and gentle. You make me laugh."

"I hate that you have memories with her of things you and I never shared."

I'm sure he knows I'm talking about sex, and my cheeks flush slightly. He said we're only friends, so why I'm pushing him to tell me about their sexual history, I have no idea. I sound like a jealous girlfriend, but I'm unable to stop myself.

Colton leans in toward me, his dark eyes pinning me in place. "Do you want to know why I only wanted oral sex with you?"

I nod, unable to resist the nugget of information he's dangling in front of me.

"Because, that's something Stella wouldn't do."

"What are you saying?"

"I never fucked her mouth. I never completely lost myself with her. Each time with you – it was just us.

There were no bitter memories to taint that. It was our thing."

His words send a rush of conflicting emotions skittering through me. My heartbeat thrums in my chest as I remember our erotic encounters with vivid clarity. "She wouldn't…Why?"

He shrugs. "Said she didn't like the taste. Of course, that's exactly what I caught her doing to the gardener – deep throating him in the library. She seemed to like it just fine – as long as it wasn't with me."

My heart aches for him. As pissed as I am, I'm beginning to understand the deep hurt and mistrust he's carried around with him. I recall how he never seemed to want to go into that room and my heart softens just a bit. And I do like knowing that as trivial as it is, going down on him was something only I did. I guess I now understand his aversion to the library too.

"Being with her was a mere convenience. You are

a choice. One I desperately want to make – if you'll let me."

His words rattle me. I shouldn't trust him – not after he lied about his past – made me believe he was single. Yet, there's no denying part of me still wants him. "But you said friends." My voice is tiny. It would take little to no effort on his part to convince me we'd be better as more than friends. The heat buzzing between us is palatable and intense.

"For now, yes. I want you to trust me again. I won't push you yet."

Yet. That word rings loudly in my head. I swallow heavily, trying to decipher the deeper meaning behind his words. He wants me back, I'm sure of it. So why in the hell won't he just divorce Stella and move on with his life? Two years of waiting her out seems extreme. Even for someone as stubborn and cocky as Colton.

"I'm sorry…" I apologize, though I'm not entirely sure for what. I just hate the thought of Colt finding that witch on her knees, giving to another man what she withheld from him.

"Don't be," he says, coolly. But his eyes tell a different story. They're dark and faraway, as if he's fighting to escape the sour memories that follow him around the rooms of his own house.

I leave Colton to his work and find myself wandering the rooms of his house, ending in the library. I hate Stella. I can't say I've ever really hated anyone before, I hate Becca's cancer, I hate that Colton is married, but I absolutely fucking *hate* Stella. She's made a man who is so sweet under his hardened exterior question himself and his relationships. I stand there in the library, silently staring off into space for far too long.

When I find Colton in his office later, I convince him to leave his work for the night and get some sleep.

The dark circles under his eyes tug at something inside me, but I resist the urge to wrap my arms around his neck. He is not mine to soothe.

We part ways at the top of the stairs and say goodnight. The walk to the guest room feels too long and just odd. As I crawl in between the cool sheets, my thoughts are squarely on the man down the hall.

***

The following day is interesting. A strange sense of unease grows as the day passes. We eat our meals together, I go for a jog, and Colton works at the kitchen island while I flip through a magazine, but I can't help but feel something is off. We're struggling to find our rhythm as just friends. I keep stealing glances at him, noticing the way his white t-shirt clings to his sculpted chest and I feel his eyes on my backside when I walk away. I hate that I can't touch him.

Is it even possible to be friends with a man I want so desperately?

When night falls, I've showered and brushed my teeth and done my regular nightly ritual, but I'm anything but ready for bed. My body is wound too tight. I'm beginning to think this new arrangement I've agreed to will never work.

After tossing and turning for an hour, I decide to go to Colton. I know my actions – going into his bedroom in the middle of the night – will define how we spend our next several months, but I don't care. I need to see him, to talk to him, to understand what I'm getting myself into.

I creep down the hallway on tiptoes like a stealthy intruder and tap gently on his door.

No response.

Maybe he's already asleep.

I let myself in and my eyes search out the

darkened room. His blankets are in a messy heap on the bed, but I don't see any movement.

"Colton?" I whisper.

Nothing.

I creep closer and kneel at the edge of the mattress. Now that my eyes have adjusted to the pitch darkness, I can see he's not here. The room is quiet and empty.

A pang of disappointment, followed by curiosity flares inside me.

I venture off in search of him.

Chapter Five

Sophie

Nightfall has bathed the house in near total blackness, save for the little path lights that are strategically placed in outlets throughout the home. It's just enough light for me to see as I navigate the stairs and head toward Colton's office. I pass the den on my way and confirm he's not in there. Perhaps he couldn't sleep either and he's gotten up to work. His blankets were strewn across his bed like he'd fought with them. My guess is that he attempted sleep, just like me, and lost the battle.

His office door is open and a lamp provides a swath of soft light. I hear grunting sounds and my stomach lurches.

I step around the doorway and I'm utterly

shocked at what I find.

Colton is sitting in his leather chair, his pants are undone and his thick cock is standing proudly. His hand is moving up and down in short, uneven strokes and he's grunting softly.

My pussy clenches at the sight of him. I release a tiny whimper and his eyes snap up to mine.

"Christ, Sophie." He tucks himself back inside his pants, which is not an easy task. He's rock hard and his engorged cock does not look happy to be stuffed into the confined space. I wince just watching him.

"Don't you fucking knock?" he barks in my direction.

"The door was open," I murmur, feeling idiotic.

He looks behind me to the open doorway. "I suppose it was. What are you doing out of bed though?"

"I think the better question is, what are you?" I feel cheeky and want to watch him squirm a bit at being caught. Except he's collected and composed, and continues watching me calmly.

He shakes his head at me, obviously not taking the bait. "Don't ask questions that you're not prepared to hear the answers to."

I'm not sure what he means, but I cross the room and stand before him, my legs still shaky from what I just witnessed. "You were pleasuring yourself."

He's quiet and still.

I hadn't meant it as an accusation, but thankfully Colton doesn't seem to take offense. "I'm just curious…"

"I have needs, Sophie, as you know."

I nod. "We both do." I take a step closer.

"Be careful, sweetness. You're playing with fire, tempting me, making me want something I can't have."

"Who says you can't?" I don't know who the girl is taunting him, but I'm feeling bold and restless and lonely. It's a piss poor combination, and makes me want to act out.

He lifts one dark eyebrow, watching me closely. "Did you change your mind about all this, because I'll fuck you here and now, so deep you'll still feel my cock inside you tomorrow."

I don't say anything else, mostly because I don't know what to say, but my body is humming with anticipation. My nipples harden against the flimsy tank top and my panties cling to my sensitive folds.

Colton releases a frustrated groan and pushes his palm against his erection – which is definitely still there. "What in the actual fuck, Sophie?" His tone is a cross between playful and angry.

"I'm sorry I interrupted you," I say.

"Fuck it," he says, leaning his head back against the leather chair and closing his eyes.

When he opens them again, his anger is gone. All I see is lust.

"Why didn't you ever take me?" I ask.

"As the weeks passed, you started to mean more to me. I didn't want to take something from you that wasn't mine."

It is yours, I want to tell him. "But that day that Stella showed up, you were going to." I'd seen the look of resolve in his eyes and I knew he was finally going to give himself to me.

"Because I knew in that moment you belonged to me. Even without the auction, without the agreement. You were mine."

I watch his eyes, not disagreeing in the slightest. *I still am.*

The way his dark gaze sweeps over to mine tells me he wants me, yet he's choosing not to push me. I want to know why. "Why did you suggest we be just friends?" I ask.

He takes a deep breath and lets it out slowly. Then

he motions for me to sit down in one of the chairs across from his desk.

I follow his lead and sit, tucking my bare legs underneath me. The tank top and pajama short set I'm wearing is no match against the cool air conditioning. Either that or my body is still trembling from what I witnessed when I walked in.

"I was developing real feelings for you, something that scared the fuck out of me given my past."

"I don't understand. We were both falling…" It's the first time I've admitted my true feelings, but something tells me this is no surprise to him.

Colton doesn't say anything, he just patiently watches me like we have all night to sit here and speak in riddles. Perhaps his *just friends* speech was only that – a hollow request made only to get me to stay.

"If you want a real shot with me, I need a few things from you," he says.

"Such as?"

"You know I've been burned before when it comes to women, and money and trust."

"Yes," I acknowledge.

"Women usually only want me for my money," he adds.

"What does that have to do with me?" I am the furthest thing from a gold digger there is.

"Well, you have to admit the start to our relationship doesn't exactly instill confidence. You only agreed to go with me that night because I was paying you."

"Yes, but as I got to know you, you know it wasn't about the money. That money was for Becca. I told you I'll give you the rest back right now."

"That's not what I want." His tone is adamant and I feel like we're spinning in circles.

"What do you want then?"

"Something much more valuable…" His eyes trace a path along my exposed cleavage, making my nipples harden.

I remain quiet, waiting expectantly and wondering what he has in mind.

"I want to know I can trust you. I need your faith and belief in me that I'll handle my past."

"You can trust me…" I start.

"Talk is cheap and I've been burned before. What happened with Stella makes it hard for me to believe in women, Sophie. Lack of judgment and one broken marriage under my belt may be understandable, but two? That's not something I'm willing to risk. Friends is safer right now."

"You don't trust me?"

He doesn't respond.

"You're the one who concealed the truth," I blurt.

"That may be, but you wanted to know how I felt

and I'm telling you," he says.

"I don't know what you're trying to tell me," I admit. "You have to know that I'm nothing like her, Colton." I hate that one wicked woman has ruined it for the rest of us.

The look he gives me is incredulous. "You're only in my life because of monetary reasons. I paid you to be here, and you ran out on me as soon as things got tough. What am I supposed to think?" he says, pinning me with a heated glare.

God, he's right. When I look at my actions through that lens, I can see what he means. I was only here because of the money. As soon as I was confronted with his past, I ran out on him, refusing to listen to a single word.

"I need to be able to trust the woman that I'm with," he adds.

It wrecks me to see our arrangement through his

eyes, to know that he viewed me as another woman only interested in his wealth. I stand and fold my arms over my chest. Why I'd ever thought this friends only thing was a good idea, I have no clue. "This isn't going to work for me. I want you. You want me. Yet you don't trust women. And I can't just overlook your marriage. We're at an impasse."

"So it seems." Colton drums his fingers on his desk.

Standing there in the quiet solitude of his office, I wonder what in the world I'll do now. I consider packing my bags and going home, but deep down inside, I know that's not the solution. I'd be doing exactly what Colton expects. Running away. I need to stay and show him there's a different way. Even if it scares the ever loving crap out of me.

An idea takes hold and I'm unable to shake it away. My mouth starts working before my brain can even catch up with what I'm proposing. "I have moral standards. Ones that dictate I don't sleep with married men."

He watches me curiously.

I sit down in front of him once again and take a calming breath. "I want to prove to you that you can trust me. That you can put your faith in a woman again."

"How?"

"By putting myself aside and submitting to you like I should have done from the first day you bought me."

Hungry eyes flash on mine. "I don't understand."

"I'm scared, Colt. Of all of this. My feelings for you, of being hurt, of giving you my virginity. I'm scared you won't sever ties with Stella. But I have faith in you. This is my way of showing you that I trust you to do the right thing and the best way I can prove to you that I'm not going anywhere is to give myself to you."

"Sophie…" he groans, rubbing a hand through his

hair.

"You can have me any way you want me."

"You can't mean that."

I nod slowly, letting my offer sink in. "Anything you want."

"I want your virginity, sweetness. I want total claim over you. It's the only way to show me that you're really here for me."

"But you said friends," I tease, lightly, drawing out the delicious verbal sparring that is so much like foreplay.

"Fuck being friends. I want to be inside you."

"I want that too," I say. "More than anything."

"You sure about that?"

I nod, meeting his dark gaze. "There was a man I met at a bar in Italy, he was attractive and polite and…"

"Did you want to fuck him, Sophie? Did you want him to put his cock inside of you?"

His possessive side makes me feel warm and

flustered. "Just listen," I admonish. "I could have slept with him, and in fact Becca encouraged it. She said still being a virgin was my choice and I could have gone through with it."

"But you didn't?"

I shake my head. "I knew it should be you. I want it to be you."

He rises to his feet and pulls me up against him. My chest is flush with his and his arms wrap around my middle, crushing me to him. It steals my breath and I stand there, motionless, letting him hold onto me for dear life. The move is surprisingly tender, and I can tell my offer has struck something within him.

I can't think of a single thing to say, but I know with resounding clarity this isn't something that can be spoken. He needs to see my actions to understand where my loyalties lay. Just as I'm contemplating my next move, he lays his head on my shoulder, resting his cheek against the top of my breast. I can feel his breath ghosting over my nipples in soft pants. My skin heats with the nearness of him, but this isn't sexual. It's a sweet gesture, like he's acknowledging my acceptance of him and all his baggage.

I begin to wrap my arms around him, but he stops me, taking my hands and holding them at my sides, linking his fingers with mine. He lifts his head from my shoulder, looking me straight in the eye. Our palms are pressed together and neither of us says a word. It feels intimate and familiar.

I hate how damaged he is, and I'm only just understanding the full depth of it in this moment. He's normally so assured, so demanding, that this tender side of him is completely unexpected.

Our eyes remain locked together and it's as if both of us are sharing the same thought. We're taking one giant step forward as a couple, each baring ourselves. Him, learning to trust again, and me throwing caution to the wind with a married man. Even without the contract, he owns me, and I'd been foolish to think I could just walk away. I am his.

Bowing his head to mine, he presses a soft kiss to my lips. My eyes lazily drift closed and I part my lips, accepting him. His tongue strokes mine, inviting me to play.

After several minutes of his deep, hungry kisses, I pull away, breathless. "You said it's been two years. That's a long time to wait."

He swallows, his adam's apple bobbing. His hands unlink from mine and travel up my arms to cup my face. "What game are you playing?" he asks, a confused edge to his voice.

"No games. Just us. You need to be able to trust the woman you're with."

"Of course," he agrees.

"I'm yours, sir. Anything you want. The kinkiest

thing you can dream up." I gaze up at him, meaning every word. I feel naughty and sexual and I like it. I've laid myself bare and I have no idea what he's thinking.

"If I want to bend you over and fuck you until you're raw?"

The hungry edge to his voice is unmistakable. I want to fulfill his every desire and ease this tension between us more than I want my next breath. "Anything you want," I murmur.

"And if I want to take your tight little ass?"

My stomach flips, but my eyes remain on his. I don't know if he's trying to scare me, or if that's something he actually desires. Straightening my shoulders, I respond. "Then I'm game. I believe in you. And I believe in us."

"Are you sure about this? Because once I'm buried inside you, I won't be able to stop."

"I'm sure." *At least I think I am.* "When do we start?" I ask.

"Now."

His harsh tone startles me. And the heat in the room seems to ratchet up several degrees. "Do you want my mouth?" I ask, lowering myself to my knees on the plush carpeting.

"No." He gazes down at me, and strokes my cheek with his thumb. "As tempting as this pretty little mouth of yours is, I need to fuck you."

A gasp out a strangled breath. I'd forgotten how explicit he could be about his needs. The sweet tender Colton is gone. The man standing before me is all masculine strength and domineering presence.

I swallow and give a tight nod.

Colton

Sophie doesn't know that I've already signed the divorce papers, but her trust in me means everything. I knew my instincts were right about her. Not only is she every man's wet dream come true, but she has a heart of gold too. She understands my trust issues and she's going out on a limb in the only way she knows how to prove to me that she's here for the right reasons. I almost want to weep when I realize it.

Sophie waits anxiously on her hands and knees, completely naked before me. Her complete trust in me is staggering and unexpected. It ignites all kinds of feelings I thought I'd sworn off long ago.

The night has certainly taken a turn for the better. After a heated phone call with Stella, I'd crawled into bed alone. I lay there unable to sleep and realized I was being incredibly fucking childish. I'd shucked off the blankets and ventured to my office to review the documents from my attorney that had been sitting in my inbox for far too long. I'd printed them and stared down at them for an eternity, my head buzzing and heart aching. I'd signed them on the spot, the weight on my chest lifting almost immediately.

Why in the world I'd told Sophie that I would be her friend, I had no clue. I was wound so tight that before I even knew it, I had my cock in my hand when Sophie found me. And now she kneels before me, her ass turned up and her hands buried in the plush carpeting of my office. I walk around her and see her spine stiffen.

"Relax, sweetness," I say. "You promised me anything I wanted," I remind her.

I come to a stop behind her and am pleased to see her pussy glistening with dewy moisture. I haven't laid a hand on her yet – I just ordered her to strip, and she had, baring herself to me completely before falling to her hands and knees at my command. It's a fucking beautiful sight and my cock aches at the thought of finally taking her. But I won't rush tonight.

I stand over her and slowly unbutton my shirt, discarding it to the floor with her clothes. I can feel Sophie's eyes watching my movements, her head turned back to look at me. Knowing she's watching and that she's every bit as turned on as I am fuels me. Her eyes burn straight through me, creating a physical ache. I take my time, unlatching my belt and pull it slowly from my pants. Opening the front of my dress pants, I push my boxers down my hips and take my cock in my right hand. I don't need to look up to know she's zeroed in on my every move.

She watches me stroke myself in long, even pulls, her eyes tracing every hard inch of me.

"Are you ready for me, sweet girl?" I ask.

Her eyes dart up to mine and she gives a wordless nod.

I drop to my knees, positioning myself behind her and place my hands on the rounded curve of her ass cheeks. Using my thumbs, I part her lower lips and find her wet and ready.

Now that is a fucking turn on. I haven't even touched her yet and my angel is soaking wet for me.

I position myself at her entrance and tease her with the tip of my cock, gliding it back and forth. Her warmth envelopes me and the sensation makes my balls tighten against my body. *Fuuuck.* I can already tell the sex between us is going to be intense and I haven't even penetrated her yet. She's said that she wants this, but I have to be sure before I take something so precious from her. She wiggles her hips, pushing back against me and I almost lose my shit right then and there. I grip her ass and stifle a groan, watching the wide head of cock press into her pink flesh.

A shaky breath shudders across her lips. "What about a condom," she murmurs.

I pull back and resume teasing her by rubbing my dick against her. "Tonight I want to fuck you with my mouth. And if you're good, tomorrow I'll fuck you with my cock."

"And the day after that?"

"If you can still stand, yes."

She inhales sharply. "And will you fuck my ass?"

Goddamn. Hearing those erotic words fall from her perfect lips causes a drop of liquid to leak from my tip. "Not yet, beautiful. Soon, but not yet. I'll know when you're ready for more."

"Oh."

"If I do it too soon I'll hurt you," I explain.

"You'll hurt me?"

"I won't hurt you. Not on purpose. But your ass is

really tight." I give her ass cheek a playful smack.

She smirks up at me in challenge.

I spank her again, sharper this time and am rewarded with a satisfying crack and a gasp of breath as Sophie inhales.

She might think she's in control – giving herself to me this way – but I'm about to show her that I'm still very much in charge.

I lean into her, kissing the twin dimples in her lower back in that damn sexy spot just above her ass.

Moving lower, I plant my face at the juncture between her thighs.

She momentarily stiffens, realizing that my face is pretty much buried in her ass.

"Colton…" she whines. Her tone is unsure, hesitant and she fights against me, trying to wiggle out of my grasp.

"Don't," I warn and pull her hips back toward me.

She has no reason to be self-conscious around me. I want to worship her pussy with my mouth. I could stay here for hours and it wouldn't be long enough. My hands firmly hold her hips in place as my tongue sweeps out and licks her from top to bottom. She releases a soft groan and stops trying to pull away.

She tastes sweet, like candy, and I indulge, not letting up my rhythm against her clit until her moans of pleasure are loud enough to wake the neighbors.

"Colton!" she cries out again and again.

She's right there, at that beautiful moment right before her orgasm crashes through her. I plunge two fingers deep inside and feel her squeeze around me.

Suddenly it's no longer just about watching her come undone, I want her to come harder than she ever has in her life and know it's because of me.

She pushes her ass back, grinding against my fingers and a vision of her riding my dick flashes through my mind.

"That's it, baby. Let go." My teeth sink into the fleshy cheek of her perfect ass and my fingers curl upward to that sensitive spot inside.

Sophie comes undone, repeating my name again and again as she gasps for breath and clamps down on my fingers.

Her body trembles with the intensity of her release, and I pull her up from her prone position, cradling her in my arms and kissing her neck, her forehead, her lips.

"Shit, that was hot, baby."

"Colton…" she murmurs again. Her blue eyes are hazy and unfocused and she's panting like she just ran a marathon. "It's never been like that."

"That's because it's me and you," I say, meaning every word. We share an undeniable connection that goes much deeper than the physical. I don't know if it's because of all those weeks we spent living together, getting to know each other and all but ignoring the explosive chemistry between us, but it's intense and unlike anything I've ever experienced.

Our lips meet in a rush of hungry kisses. Sophie's hands fumble down my body, tracing my abs and moving lower until she finds my hard cock. She teases me at first, her fingertips exploring me, her nails scrapping lightly against my skin, her delicate hand cupping my balls. I grunt when she grips me and begins lazily stroking up and down. I push my hips up to meet her strokes.

"Harder, baby." I show her what I like, tightening my hand around hers and begin to pump faster.

Her lips momentarily still against mine as though she's concentrating on finding the rhythm. When she does, pleasure rips through my body and I move my hand to the back of her neck.

"Feels so fucking good," I groan, pushing my hands into her hair and bringing her mouth back to mine.

While our tongues collide and explore, Sophie uses both hands to stroke my length up and down until I'm ready to explode.

"Soph," I grunt. "You're gonna make me come…"

She bows her head and takes me into the warm cavern of her mouth, suckling against the head of my dick. It's unexpected and hot that she wants to taste me and I can't hold back a second longer. Tangling my fingers in her hair, I erupt in a stream of incoherent curses and empty myself into her mouth.

Sophie lets out a low moan and swallows every drop.

"Damn baby." I stare at her in stunned disbelief. I can't believe she just did that.

She smiles shyly and drops her eyes to my softening cock, then gives him a gentle pat.

"I'm glad you decided against being friends." I stroke her hair back from her face and kiss her lips.

"You knew that would never work, didn't you?"

"I knew it wasn't what I wanted, but I was willing to try if that was the only way to have you in my life." It's the honest truth.

She gazes up at me, her eyes shining bright with longing. "I want everything."

"I do too, sweet Sophie. I do too."

I rise to my feet, cradling her in my arms. "Come on, let's go to bed."

"What about our clothes?" She peers down at the heap of discarded clothes and undergarments decorating my office floor.

"It'll give the housekeepers something to gossip about."

She lays her head against my shoulder, lets out a contented sigh, and lets me carry her up the stairs.

Chapter Six

Sophie

When I wake in the morning, Colton is already up and gone from the bed. Glancing at the clock, I realize it' ten after seven, and since it's a Monday, I assume he's gotten up to get ready for work.

Wanting to see him before he starts his day, I climb from the bed and venture downstairs wearing only the t-shirt of his that I slept in. The warm cotton is soft against my skin and reminds me there are so many tiny things I missed about him. A happy smile plays at the edges of my mouth.

I find him in the kitchen, dressed in a dark suit, crisp white shirt, and a navy blue tie. His feet are still bare. He looks delicious. Maybe I'll just have him for breakfast.

His eyes lift to mine and he sets his cell phone down on the island. "Aren't you a pretty sight." His gaze wanders along the curves visible under the t-shirt, before lingering on my bare legs. "Come here."

His simple command tightens my body with anticipation. I cross the kitchen and stop in front of him. "Did you sleep okay?" I ask, reaching out to fix his tie.

"Like a fucking rock." He plants a kiss to my temple. "Thank God you're back."

I wrap my arms around his waist and exhale softly as he pulls me into his arms and holds me tight. Seeing him all buttoned up in his suit and tie makes me want to mess him up, undress him and do naughty things – right here in the kitchen.

"You said today was the day…" I lift my face into his neck and whisper against his ear, letting the words linger between us. The promise of sex later has my body entirely too aware of his nearness, his scent.

Colton's mouth tugs up in a playful smirk. "Fuck, Soph…"

I toy with the hem of my t-shirt and see his gaze drop south. Dressed in just an old gray t-shirt, and I've never felt sexier. I lift the shirt, revealing the fact I'm not wearing any panties, when Colton suddenly clears his throat, looking uncomfortable.

"What?" I ask.

He releases a sigh. "Marta's here."

Disappointment courses through me and I almost groan in frustration. I drop the hem of the shirt, covering myself once again and peek around Colton to the kitchen window, which has a direct view of the driveway. Her little red sports car is parked in the drive, but she's nowhere to be found. *Weird.*

"I'm going to get dressed," I say and leave him in the kitchen. Call me old fashioned, but when one of Colton's employees is here, I figure I should at least be wearing panties. I draw the line at removing his t-shirt though and just add undergarments and a pair of yoga pants before heading back downstairs.

I run into Marta in the hall outside of one of the guest rooms.

"Sophie?" She sounds surprised and her eyebrows rise as she takes me in.

"Hi." I peek around her and see several suitcases in the guest room and stray articles of clothing on the bed. What in the hell? I don't understand what's going on, but rather than stay and chat with Marta, I want to talk to Colton. I head straight for the kitchen.

"Marta looks pretty cozy upstairs."

"She's going to be staying here," he says, without further explanation.

"Why? Doesn't she have her own place?" If he gives me some speech about companionship or the house being empty, I am going to lose it. I was already suspicious about what all their relationship entailed and after his marriage fiasco I couldn't handle anymore bombshells of information being dropped on me at the moment.

"She has a rat infestation in her building and her condo is being restored. It's just for a few days or so."

Rats? Ew. "Okay."

"What's wrong? You seem upset."

"She just seemed surprised to see me here, like she didn't know I was back in the picture."

He shrugs. "You just came back yesterday. I haven't gotten around to telling her yet."

His response makes sense, I just don't like the idea that with Colton newly single, Marta's wasted no time in moving herself in. And judging by the three giant suitcases she brought with her, she's planning on being here for more than just a couple of days.

Marta chooses that exact moment to enter the kitchen and help herself to a coffee mug from the cupboard. I know it's irrational, but her familiarity with this man and his home bugs me. "Ready for work, boss? We can ride in together." She treats him to a wide smile.

Colton gives me a peck on the lips and his eyes implore mine to let it go before he turns to face Marta. "Actually, I figured we'd probably be working different hours, so we'd drive in separate."

"No, that's okay. I don't mind if you have to work late, I'm game for whatever. Plus, it'll be a good time for us to catch up. I can bring you up to speed on the renovations I have planned for the pool house."

"What renovations to the pool house?" I inquire.

"Colton didn't tell you?"

I shake my head.

"One of the pumps malfunctioned and the pool house flooded. I've taken over redecorating it since … never mind." Marta smiles coyly, sharing a secret look with Colt.

"Since what?" I ask.

She shrugs. "Since Stella is the one who decorated it and I didn't think the purple and gold décor went with Colton's taste, I figured it was time for a makeover."

Colton slides his warm palm against my limp one, a gesture meant to calm and reassure me. I have no idea why I'm acting so territorial over a man I'm not even sure is mine, but seeing Marta here this morning has all my senses on high alert. If I am going to have an actual relationship with Colton, I need the women of his past to stop showing up here unannounced. I make a mental note to ask Colton for details about his relationship with Marta.

I stand near the front door in my pajamas and watch as Colton and Marta climb into her little red sports car. They pull out of the gated driveway and onto the road and the sound of blaring music lingers until they disappear from sight.

I sigh and shut the door. My new life is going to take some getting used to.

Chapter Seven

Colton

As a successful entrepreneur who runs two companies, who regularly deals with top executives and negotiates with fierce competitors, I find it almost laughable how worked-up one small girl, dressed only in my t-shirt can get me. As Marta drives my thoughts drift to Sophie, as they often do.

I type out a text message to her.

I miss you already.

Her reply is almost instant.

Miss you more.

I smile and type out my reply. *We'll have fun tonight.*

You promise?

Her response makes me chuckle.

All you can handle, sweetness.

"So, Sophie's back?" Marta asks, adjusting the volume of the radio down and pulling my attention away from my phone.

I'm detecting a hint of jealously stewing between them – something I need to put a stop to right the fuck now.

"Yes, she's moved back in – for good, I hope."

Marta lowers her sunglasses and looks over at me. "Wow. That's a big step."

"Indeed," I confirm. "I'm crazy about her, Marta, and I need to know that you understand that. You and I have a complicated past, but that's where it needs to stay – in the past."

"I see." I detect a hint of disappointment in her voice.

I can't say I'm surprised by her reaction, I've long suspected she's wanted more with me.

"I value you as a friend, and an employee, but Sophie's a game changer for me. In fact, I'm finally dealing with Stella."

"I get it, Colt." Her voice takes on a slightly exasperated tone. "Things were over between us long before Sophie came into the picture. And I'm a big girl. I can deal."

"I know you can. Thank you for that." I'm glad that she seems to understand. The last thing I'd want is for things to get weird between her and Sophie. Or between her and I for that matter.

"Besides, it was only a few times," she remarks.

We both gaze out at the road and I sense that she's recalling the few times we were intimate with vivid detail.

"It's in the past," I confirm. *I just hope it stays there.* Marta doesn't respond. "It's all but forgotten, right?"

She lets out a short chuckle. "I wouldn't go that

far, Colton. I don't think I'll forget anytime soon that you're the biggest man I've ever been with or how harsh and commanding you can be when you're aroused."

Our encounters aren't as memorable in my recollections. I only recall that in the months after Stella left, I was depressed and lonely. Marta was there and willing and I allowed her to take the edge off a few times, but we never had sex. "I'm serious about this, Marta. If you make things difficult for Sophie, or if you dredge up things from the past..."

She turns to me sharply. "Relax, boss. Leave me with my fond memories and I promise not to say anything."

We share a tense ride to work and I make a mental note to tell Sophie everything tonight when I return home. Now that she's back and trusting in me to do the right thing, I won't have something so inconsequential ruining our progress.

132

The day drags by at a snail's pace as I anticipate my evening with Sophie. My brothers break up the afternoon by surprising me with lunch. Things at work have been so busy that I've been pushing off our weekly lunch date. Today they take no chances, bursting into my office with my assistant trailing behind them apologetically.

"They just barged in, sir," he says, looking troubled.

"It's okay, David."

My assistant, David, is a bit of a nerdy and frail type, and I got the sense he's overwhelmed in the presence of my brothers. But he's the best assistant I've ever had so I won't admonish him for the interruption.

"You've gotta eat," Pace says, holding up a bag of takeout from one of my favorite sushi restaurants. "And I need an update on what's going on with sweet Sophie."

He had flown to Italy with me on a whim, so perhaps I did owe him an update. "Is there a spicy tuna roll in that bag?" I ask.

He nods and begins removing the containers of food.

I join him and Collins at the large marble table in the center of my office.

"So?" Collins ask. "Was your impromptu trip to Italy wasted? Or did you get the girl?

"Sophie's moved back in," I confirm.

"Fuck yeah." Pace's wide smile lights up his entire face. He's always worn his emotions directly on his sleeve. It's both a blessing and curse. He's a real estate developer, so his gregarious personality often helps him win over clients, but can be a hindrance when he's negotiating big deals. All the cards are face up on the table with him. You can see every fleeting thought passing through his brain.

"And Stella?" Collins asks.

My older brother has been riding me for years about divorcing her. Even though he's only two years older, he's always acted more like a father-figure to both me and Pace. "I signed the papers."

Pace jumps to his feet. "Holy fucking shit! We need some goddamn champagne up in this bitch."

"Sit the fuck down," I grumble, but am unable to hide the crooked smile lifting one corner of my mouth. "Yeah, yeah, I know. It's about fucking time."

"I'm so fucking glad Sophie's in your life," Collins says, helping himself to some of the pickled ginger on my plate. It's obvious he attributes her presence in my life to this change. And of course, he's right.

"We need to celebrate, bro. Seriously," Pace says.

"It's not a horrible idea. A big bash to mark your freedom from the mega bitch," Collins says, chewing thoughtfully.

"Drop it, boys. I've signed the papers and sent them over to my lawyer. That's celebration enough." No need to celebrate the anal raping my bank account is getting just to pay her to go away.

We eat in comfortable silence for several minutes. At the lull in conversation, my mind automatically wanders to Sophie and what will happen tonight when I get home.

"Marta's single, right?" Pace asks, popping a piece of sushi into his mouth.

"Why do you ask?" I inquire, folding a napkin across my lap.

"She looks like she could use a good hard ride." He grins.

I set down my chopsticks. "Don't fuck my employees. Why is that so hard for you to understand?"

He rolls his eyes. "Fuck, dude. You're worse than a woman. First you curse me out for trying to get with Sophie's sister Becca, and now you're whining about me noticing Marta's pert little ass."

"I'm not whining. I'm pointing out that surely your pickup skills extend beyond the couple of women in my inner circle that I'd prefer not get fucked over by you and then come crying to me. I know your history with women, asshole."

Collins chimes in, coming to my defense. "He's right, dipshit, your track record is zero and what a hundred?"

"What the hell does that mean?" Pace momentarily stops chewing.

"You've had zero successful monogamous relationships and over a hundred sexual partners," Collins says.

Pace shrugs. "I stopped keeping track once I reached the triple digits."

"Listen, asshole. I told you. Marta works for me, so don't fuck her. And in regards to Becca, she has cancer.

She doesn't need any additional stress in her life from someone who will hit it once and walk away. Not to mention she's my girl's sister. If you deflower her and then pull a disappearing act, I'd have to deal with the fallout."

He sulks, sinking deeper into his chair, but doesn't retort.

Collins and I share a quick look of triumph.

I have no idea if Becca's a virgin, like Sophie is, and it doesn't matter. I don't want Pace anywhere near her. His history with women is deplorable.

"Is Sophie still a virgin?" Pace asks.

"Not for long," I confirm.

Chapter Eight

Sophie

When Colton and Marta arrive home, I'm showered, dressed and waiting in the kitchen, just opening a bottle of white wine and setting out long-stemmed glasses. I frown looking down at the third glass on the island. *Three's a crowd.*

When they enter the kitchen, Marta excuses herself, immediately going upstairs to change, leaving Colton and I all alone. *Bliss.* I've been waiting for this moment all damn day, and I don't feel like I can wait a minute longer.

He stalks over to me, looking delectable in his suit. I might have exercised restraint this morning when I barely avoided tearing it off of him, but I will show no such patience tonight.

Without saying a single word, his hands cup my cheeks and he pulls my face to his, pressing his lips to mine and giving me a long kiss. When he pulls away, I'm dizzy and filled with longing.

"How was your day?" I ask.

"Way too fucking long. I missed you," he says.

I feel the exact same way. "Would it be rude if we skipped dinner and went straight to bed?" I think about the plates in the warming tray that Beth has left for all three of us. Apparently the household staff knew Marta was staying here. Of course, as his personal assistant, Marta probably told them.

Colton runs his hands down my body, stopping at my hips and securing my body to his. "Dinner is the last thing on my mind." He's looking at me like he's already picturing me naked.

A warm shiver runs through me. I'd wondered if it

was going to bother me that Marta was here in the house for our first time, but now, I don't care if she hears me screaming down the house. She can stuff it.

"I've been hard all fucking day," Colton groans, bringing my hand down below his belt and pressing it into the gigantic bulge there. I close my hand around him and hear him grunt.

It takes every ounce of willpower I have not to drop to my knees and take him into my mouth. Even if I don't care about Marta hearing our sounds of pleasure behind closed doors, I don't want her to see my man's package. That is not something I plan on sharing. Now or ever.

His hips rock forward as my palm moves up and down over him. "I can't wait to be inside you," he whispers low near my ear.

My panties flood with moisture.

"Let's go upstairs. I'll help you change out of your

suit." I give him a playful look.

Footsteps round the corner and I know we're no longer alone. I turn to face Marta, making sure I remain in front of Colton to block the view of his raging erection. Apparently we're on the same page, because his hands circle my waist, silently communicating that I need to stay put.

My eyes wander behind her to the suitcases stacked together on the floor.

"My landlord says the mouse infestation is all cleared up, so I'm going back home," she says.

"I thought it was rats?" I ask.

"Oh, right. Mice, rats. Same thing." She smiles, but her cheeks flush slightly, knowing she's been caught in a lie.

I get the sense that she'd only been staying here in my absence to make a move on Colton, and now that I'm back, she knows she's missed her chance.

She tows her suitcases behind her, stopping to stretch up on her tiptoes and to give Colton a quick peck on the cheek. "Thanks for your hospitality. And I'm totally on board with what we talked about in the car."

He nods silently, his mouth drawn into a firm line.

A few minutes later the door closes behind her and we hear her little red sports car drive away, the noise fading into the distance until the only sounds are our heartbeats and ragged breathing.

I spin to face Colton again. He's watching me with an intense expression. "That was rude of me not to help her take her suitcases out, but I couldn't very well do that with my cock hard. What are you doing to me, baby?" he groans in frustration.

I giggle and lift up on my toes to kiss him. "I'm sure it's okay. She looked like she had them handled."

He shrugs. "I suppose she did."

"What did you guys talk about in the car?" I ask,

remembering what Marta said just before she left.

"Huh?" he asks.

"She said she was totally on board with it…" I try to jog his memory.

He runs a hand through his hair. "Come on, we need to talk."

He leads me to the den and motions for me to sit on the sofa next to him.

My belly churns with nerves. Colton's entire mood has changed. I think whatever he's going to tell me has something to do with him and Marta. I take a deep breath and prepare myself for the worst. I might have told him just yesterday that I was his and that no matter what I trusted him. Now I want to swallow all those words and curl up in a ball with the hurt that is already threatening to overtake me.

"Take a deep breath, Sophie," Colton murmurs. I'm sure he can see the hurt and worry written all over my face. "After Stella left, I had a short rebound fling with Marta," he says.

My stomach drops to my toes as my worst suspicions are confirmed. I pull another deep breath into my lungs at Colton's urging and fight to remain in control by reminding myself that it was in the past.

"I was destroyed after my divorce," he explains. "She was there and available and I regret it now, but we messed around a couple of times."

"Oh." I'm speechless and gutted and feel like crying. I've been jealous of Marta and her good looks and close relationship with Colton from day one. And now all my hunches are confirmed.

"We never had sex," he adds.

This news makes me feel marginally better. "What did she mean earlier? What did you guys talk about in the car that she was on board with?"

"I told her that I'm fucking crazy about you. And

while she's known for a long time that I'm not interested in her, I let her know that I wouldn't tolerate anything getting in the way of you and I. Good employees are hard to find, but if she tried to interfere in any way…"

He leaves the rest unspoken. Geez, he'd threatened to fire her if she made things difficult for me and him?

Her cryptic message and then hightailing it out of here today must mean that she accepts Colton's relationship with me and has no intention of interfering.

"I wanted to be honest with you about my past. I want a real future with you, Soph. Tell me how you're feeling," he says.

"I'm glad you opened up and told me about Marta." But deep down I know the issue with Marta is the least of my worries. I can accept his need for a rebound fling. Growing bold, I straighten my spine. "But if you wanted a real relationship with me, you wouldn't be holding up your own divorce. And don't give me this guilty crap about money for the Africa project – if your finances were in that precarious a state, would you have really spent a million on a sex slave, oh excuse me, I mean mistress? By the sounds of it, Marta is not someone you had true feelings for, and I can get over it, but if you want this with me, you're going to have to show me that I'm worth the risk. I can't share you with Stella."

"You'll never share me." His dark eyes implore mine, possessive and filled with longing.

"I am sharing you – the memory of her scowling at me in the pool and telling me to get off her property is firmly branded into my mind. Did you notice that I can't even go near the pool?"

"Sophie, I signed the papers. Last night in my office, when you interrupted me," he says.

"WHAT?"

"Yes. It's done. I emailed them to my attorney this

morning."

"Why didn't you tell me?" This is earth-shattering news and he's mentioning it in casual conversation like's no big deal.

"I didn't want to interrupt our fun last night." He smirks.

I remembered in vivid detail our steamy encounter in his office last night where I'd pledged to give myself to him. Everything comes rushing back at once, and my belly tightens into a knot.

"Besides, everything you said, the way you laid yourself bare, your complete faith and trust in me – that was exactly what I needed. And if you'd known I'd signed the papers before you told me all that, it wouldn't have had the same impact," Colton continues.

I see what he means. I'd basically agreed to have blind faith in him to do the right thing, and it turns out, he already had. My heart swells with happiness.

"Colton…"

His eyes swing over to mine and he gives me a small smile.

When I ask about the terms of the divorce, he doesn't hold anything back. He tells me that his net worth of three hundred and sixty five million dollars was divided exactly in half. And as happy as I am about his divorce being finalized, I hate the idea that his now ex-wife is receiving even a dime from him. She'd already stripped him of his trust in women and soured his home with her memories.

Colton had pledged to spend five hundred million dollars in Africa over the next ten years, but I see now that can't happen. My heart is heavy for him, and I work to convince him that his time and donations are still more than generous. He nods and pats my knee, but I can tell his thoughts are faraway.

A few somber seconds pass, and I can tell he's

realizing there's new direction to his life. Turning over a new leaf, and all that. He's been through so much, and despite his strength and demeanor, I know it's been tough for him. I want to comfort him, to hold him. The urge to crawl into his lap is too strong to ignore and so I do.

"Sophie?" he asks.

"Just hold me," I say.

He does. Colton wraps me in his arms and holds me tight, his masculine scent enveloping me in warmth. I can tell that whatever comes next for us is going to be big. We may have started this journey together, thinking it'd be something fleeting and sexual, but the intensity of our relationship and depth of feelings are way too strong to ignore.

"What did you do today?" He brushes my hair back from my face and peers down at me where I'm still curled on his lap.

"Besides wait for my man to get home?"

"Your man?"

"My man." My voice is sure and steady. He is mine, and I won't be scared off by his admissions about Marta or his rocky past. "I went for a jog, showered, and then spent the afternoon moving my things from the guest room back into the master suite."

"Good." He continues stroking my hair and it feels lovely.

"It got me thinking though."

"About?" He nuzzles into my neck, inhaling my scent and treating me to a tender kiss on that sensitive spot just behind my ear. He's trying to distract me, and it almost works, but I know I need to have this conversation with him before things go any farther.

"You shared that room with her," I say.

Sensing the direction I'm going, Colton takes my hand in his. "I had the entire room redone when she left. The furniture, the mattress, the linens are all new."

"Did Marta pick them?" I wonder out loud, remembering her comment about redecorating the pool house.

"No. She showed me a design website and I picked everything I wanted, and then had her order it on my credit card."

"Oh."

"Does that help?"

"Yes, it does. I think I would have felt strange being intimate in the same bed you shared with your wife," I admit.

"Ex-wife," he corrects me. "And I promise you that Stella will be the furthest thing from my mind when I finally take you."

A warm ripple of heat passes between us at the mention of sex. "Did I ruin the night by asking all these questions?" I ask, meeting his blue stare.

"No. I want to be upfront with you about

152

everything from now on."

"I think I can handle that."

He cups my face with his warm palms, and traces his thumb along my lower lip. "Thank fucking God you're still here with me. Most women would have run away screaming obscenities at me, you know?"

I nod. "Yes, it's a good thing you're cute."

"You think I'm cute?" He lifts one eyebrow, watching me with scrutiny.

"Adorable," I confirm.

He shakes his head at me, his expression turning serious.

"What's wrong with that?" I ask.

"Men don't want to be called adorable Sophie."

"No?"

"No."

"What would you like to be called, Colton?"

His tongue traces his lower lip as he thinks it over.

"Tough, badass, a sex god." He gives me a playful smile and settles his hands on my waist.

"Well I wouldn't know about that last one, now would I?" I tease. His eyes latch onto mine and he gives me the most dark, hungry, aching look that I can feel deep inside my body. "Colt…"

A sound of need rumbles in his chest and his mouth comes crashing down on mine. All of the weeks of letting the sexual tension build to exquisite proportions come barreling down on us in an instant. I'm filled with lust and desire so strong that it demands immediate attention.

I'm still planted on his lap and I grind against him, writhing, fighting to get closer as he kisses me deeply. His tongue strokes mine in the most hypnotic rhythm, reminding me of the wicked way he licked my core last night until I came so hard I almost blacked out.

Feeling the hard ridge of his erection, I push my

hips closer, angling my body so that I can feel him right between my thighs. I rub myself against him wantonly.

"Colt…" I groan again, my voice a hoarse plea in the otherwise silent room.

He strips my shirt off over my head, and his hands are suddenly everywhere at once, unsnapping my bra and flinging it across the room, caressing my breasts, gently pinching my nipples. He kisses a wet path down my throat and takes one breast into his hot mouth. I cry out in a mix of pleasure and frustration. As nice as his attention on my breasts is, it's not where I need him.

"I can't fucking wait any longer, Sophie," he moans.

"Don't wait," I pant.

I reach between us and undo his belt, pushing my hands inside his pants until I find what I'm looking for. His cock is warm and weighty in my hands. God, I've missed this thing. Last night feels like so long ago, or maybe it's just that twenty-four hours without touching him is hell.

Colton shoves his pants and boxers down his hips, letting me massage his length up and down and growling out expletives.

He lifts me suddenly, setting me on my feet and making quick work of stripping me out of my pants. My panties are torn from my body next and I am almost shaking with need. Colton tugs his shirt off and kicks the pants and boxers off that are tangled around his ankles. When we're both free of our clothes, I drop to my knees, unable to resist the urge to take him into my mouth.

I swirl my tongue around his tip before planting my hands firmly around his base and sucking him deep into my mouth.

"Fuck, Sophie…" he moans, pushing his hands into my hair and rocking forward to thrust deeper.

After he admitted that it was something *she* never

did for him, it's only made me want to do it even more. It's *our* thing, and I love that.

I pump my hands up and down, licking and sucking with an increasing tempo. I've never wanted anything in my life as badly as I want his cock right now. I feel crazed with desire.

Colton cups one hand around my jaw, and moves my mouth off of him. I look up, wondering what I've done wrong.

"I need to be inside you," he growls, his voice rough with need.

He offers me his hand and I rise to my feet. I practically crawl up his body as Colton lifts me from the floor. I wrap my legs around his waist and he carries me from the room, and at first I think he's heading for the stairs, but then he stops and anchors us with my back pressed up against the wall. He rocks his thick erection against my center, teasing me and making me ache for him.

157

He kisses my neck, my lips, the tops of my breasts all while rocking his hips against me and nudging his wide tip against me.

"Can't wait…" he says. "I've been dreaming of this moment since I first saw you on that stage. Your beauty, your courage…you are so damn sexy, baby."

"Fuck me, Colton," I groan in frustration.

He reaches between us and grips his cock, sliding it through my wetness and positioning himself right at my opening. Knowing we're not going to make it to the bedroom is a huge turn-on.

"This might hurt a little at first."

"It's okay." I'm ready. I've wanted this for far too long. I'm not going to let a little discomfort ruin the experience. I can't wait to be filled with him, to see what kind of lover he is. I've imagined it for so long, I'm dying to see how he fucks. Hard and fast or long, slow strokes.

"Shit," he curses.

"What's wrong?"

"I don't have a condom."

His house is too damn big and there's no way I'm waiting while we traipse through his mansion in search of protection. Plus I realize with absolute certainty that I don't want anything between us for my first time. I want to feel him. Just me and him, without any barrier between us. "No, no condom. I want to feel you. Please, Colton."

His gaze snaps to mine and I can read the indecision in his eyes. "Are you sure?"

I nod. "Yes, just take me."

I'm sure he knows I'm not on any birth control, but I can see the exact moment he decides it doesn't matter. His eyes soften and his deep blue gaze settles on mine.

"Kiss me, sweet Sophie," he murmurs.

I do.

He widens his stance, bringing one hand under my

butt and with the other, he positions his throbbing cock against me. I cling to him with my arms wrapped tightly around his neck and my mouth fused to his.

With gentle strokes, Colton begins to move, teasing my opening with just the tip of him. I gasp when I feel him finally thrust forward. His face is a mask of concentration, like all his focus is on controlling himself so as not to hurt me. I know he's big, but in that moment, I just don't care. I want to be filled with him, to be overcome with sensation and know it's because of this man. Even if I scream out in pain, even if I bleed, it will be worth it, because it will mean he is finally making me his – a moment I've waited a lifetime for.

"Are you ready?"

I give a tight nod.

"Don't hold your breath."

I didn't know I had been, but I draw a deep inhale and Colton rocks forward, the blunt head of him penetrating me just slightly before he retreats again.

"Was that okay?" he grounds out.

"It feels good," I confirm.

There's the sensation of being stretched and just the slightest sting. It's incredible and despite the discomfort, I never want him to stop.

His tongue strokes mine as he presses inside me in tiny increments.

"God, baby…" He inches forward again, my body stretching around him.

"Colton…" I moan. "I like it."

"Good. I'm trying to make it good for you."

Realizing I'm pinned against the wall and he's holding up my entire weight, I suddenly worry that he's not enjoying this as much as I am. "Am I too heavy?"

"Don't worry about that." He inches forward again and kisses my lips. "I like holding you while I fuck you."

161

Oh. I like it too. I feel small and possessed by him in a way I never knew I craved. But I know he's taking it easy on me, rocking forward ever so carefully and then easing back every time I feel him begin to sink deeper. I know how big he is, so I thought there would be a feeling of him deeper inside me. "Does it feel as good for you?"

"Better," he confirms and a hot shiver races down my spine at the low way the word rolls off his tongue. He's so sexy and in complete control, and those two little things are my undoing. "You're clenched so snug and tight around me. Your warmth feels incredible."

I let out a groan of bliss as he inches forward again, rocking deeper this time. I've never given thought to what it would feel like to him, but I love the way he's described it.

"Fuck, you're so tight baby. This next part might hurt a little. Stay with me, okay?"

I nod and met his eyes. I can instantly see that he's

been holding back. But I also know that I trust him.

He slams his hips forward into me, filling me so completely, he steals my breath. Only a weak groan escapes. This moment is everything I've been waiting for and it's even more meaningful than I could have ever imagined. A twinge of pain deep inside dissipates after a moment.

"Fuck," he grunts. "Breathe for me, sweetness."

I pull in a deep gasp of air and cling to his shoulders as Colton pounds into me in long hard strokes, taking whatever was left of my virginity.

His steady pace continues, pushing into me and pulling back. Soon the sting subsides and I'm left with a warm pleasurable sensation, like a vessel being filled after a long drought. It's a long awaited moment that I'm incredibly glad I've saved just for him.

I squeeze my inner muscles around him, teasing a raspy groan from his throat. A few more deep thrusts that link his body deep within mine and I feel all his muscles tighten.

Done holding back, his grip tightens on my hips and he thrusts forward in fast hard strokes.

Colton brings his lips to mine and his warm, humid breath comes in fast pants as he releases a short moan of pleasure that I know must mean he's climaxing. He sinks even deeper inside me and I feel the rush of hot semen erupt within me and moments later Colton is lowering me to my feet, kissing my mouth, telling me how perfect I am. And in that moment, I feel perfect. I feel like a fucking sex goddess who just rocked her man's world. And the sleepy, satisfied look overtaking his face is beautiful.

"Sorry that was so fast. You were too much for me to handle myself properly." He kisses my neck, nuzzling into me. "Beautiful girl," he murmurs against my throat.

"It was perfect, Colton." I didn't come, but I hadn't expected to my first time.

"It wasn't perfect. But it will be. I'll train your body to come with mine," he says, dropping another kiss to my lips.

A warm shiver runs through me at the thought of orgasming in tandem with him. The image it conjures is incredibly erotic.

Before I can question what he's doing, Colton drops to his knees, brings his hot mouth to my core, and his lips latch on, sucking against my clit while his fingers push deep inside of me.

Oh dear God.

"Colt! What are you doing?" My legs tremble as my body reacts to his hot mouth owning me. "You just came in me and now you're..."

"Baby, I need to taste what's mine."

Unable to resist, I watch him with wide-eyes, and

my mouth hanging open. He is beautiful. Dark messy hair, eyelashes that flutter against his cheeks, a full lush mouth that is currently devouring me... I'm swollen with arousal and his mouth is hot and greedy, licking and sucking against me as I moan and grind myself against his face. "Colton," I murmur, my fingers sinking into his hair.

The vision of him dropping to his knees after sex and eating at me greedily is one I'll never forget. He doesn't seem to care that his own juices are dripping from my body, his only concern is my pleasure–it's incredibly hot. I draw in a shuddering breath, continuing to watch his mouth against me. His tongue lashes brutally against my clit and teases it repeatedly.

He presses two long fingers inside me, and the sight of his semen coating his fingers as they pump in and out of me is my undoing. I begin to shake and I know that my climax is close.

He grunts and nips at my clit with his teeth,

coaxing a low moan from my throat. I tighten around his fingers as my orgasm builds and I come with a shout, my legs almost giving out. Colton keeps me from collapsing in a heap, his hands locking onto my hips keeping me steady while he finishes, softly kissing my lower lips until I stop shaking. Then he rises to his feet with a smug look of satisfaction on his face.

He takes my hand and leads me from the den that I'll forever remember as the first room we've christened.

Colton doesn't stop touching me once as we make our way up the stairs and into the master bath, keeping his hand in mine, or resting innocently at my hip, or not so innocently against my backside. He only releases me to turn on the faucet to begin filling the big tub that I've missed in my time away.

"How about a relaxing soak?" he asks, kissing my lips.

"Only if you're planning to join me."

He smiles at me wickedly. "Absolutely."

We're both still as naked as the day we were born and I can't help but steal glances at his body. He's like a solid stone wall of muscle built for maximum pleasure. Deeply cut abdominal muscles that lead down into a V at his sides. My gaze drifts lower and I see his manhood is hanging heavily between his powerful thighs. Even in its relaxed state, it's impressive. The times before – when I'd pleasured him orally, he was hard again in an instant. Perhaps this time I've actually satisfied him. Quenched his thirst, so to speak. My lips twitch in a smile.

"What's so funny?" he looks down at his penis and back up at me with a frown.

"Nothing." I straighten my mouth, losing the smile.

"Sophie," he chastises. "You were looking down at my dick and laughing."

"I didn't laugh," I correct him.

"Fine, then you were smiling at him like the two of you were sharing some inside joke. Everything good between the two of you?"

"Very much so," I confirm.

"Then tell me what he did to make you smile."

"He's soft."

Colton frowns and lets out a sigh. "That tends to happen after a man ejaculates, Sophie."

I giggle, unable to stop myself. Hearing Colton say the word ejaculate has brought out my inner twelve-year-old boy. Pulling myself to together, I explain, "Yes, I know that. But the times before, the times I, um, used my mouth, he was hard again right away."

He watches me closely, his face impassive, but I can tell he's thinking about how to answer. "I tend to have a pretty quick recovery time, but you're right, with you it was insane. Honestly, I think it's because I wanted you so badly that I was constantly ready to go."

169

"And now, because of what we did downstairs you're satisfied?"

"For the moment."

Oh. I chew on my lip, realizing that just because we've already had sex once tonight doesn't mean it won't happen again. A pang of nerves hits me, as I contemplate if I'll be able to keep up with this man sexually.

"Get into the bath, sweetness," he says, drawing me from my thoughts.

Accepting his hand, I step into the tub and lower myself into the deliciously hot water. It's almost too warn, but it feels good against my overused and achy muscles. I scoot to one end of the oblong tub and Colton gets in and sits down in the water directly across from me.

"How do you feel?" he asks, his tone is soft and tender and his toes are touching mine underneath the water.

My inner tissues feel slightly swollen and tender.

But in the best possible way, I decide. "Like a woman," I smile.

He laughs out loud at me. His laughter is the best sound. He's a serious man, often quite thoughtful and composed, so hearing his burst of masculine laughter in the quiet room fills me with a deep sense of happiness.

We settle into the warm water, each of us sinking down to our shoulders and just watching the other quietly. It's a heavy moment, but in a good way. Everything we've shared, everything that's ahead of us leaves me feeling happy and secure.

"I shouldn't have come inside you, Soph. I was being careless," Colton says, finally breaking the silence.

My little happy bubble is momentarily burst. "I wanted you to."

"But you're not on birth control, are you? You could get pregnant."

"I know." I stare right back at him, waiting to see

how he'll respond.

His answer is a lazy smile that lights up his entire face. "Understood."

My body floods with endorphins and warm sensation spreads over me. He and I are on the exact same page. This is not some fling. This is not something fleeting or temporary. There is meaning and depth and complete clarity to what we are doing.

"Come here," he commands, his voice low and gravelly.

I practically swim across the tub to reach him and Colton grins as he watches me. I climb into his lap, settling against him. I open my legs and place one on either side of his hips, resting my arms on his shoulders. He cups my cheeks and brings his mouth to mine in a sweet kiss.

"Thank you for tonight. For believing in me. For giving yourself to me."

I nod slowly, letting the weight of this moment,

and the deep meaning behind his words sink in.

"You were so trusting to come home with me that night. So strong," he says, nuzzling his mouth against my throat.

"I knew out of all those men there that night that I was meant to go with you," I say.

"You belong with me. Always."

"Yes."

There are no games, no playing coy or denying our feelings and I fucking love it.

As we kiss and cuddle in the warm water, I can feel Colton's manhood lengthen and grow.

I slide up and down on him, teasing us both with the thought that he could so easily sink into me with the aid of the water.

Letting his hands drift down, he squeezes my breasts, caressing them with light touches.

"I'll never tire of this," he says.

"Of what?"

"Touching you, knowing you're mine."

I feel the exact same way and I never want this moment to end.

Colton

The first time we made love we were a tangle of limbs, desperate and fighting to get closer. This time, I'm holding her in my arms, both of us stretched out on my bed laying side by side, and I vow to take my time.

I sweep her hair back from her eyes and peer down at her. "I shouldn't have taken your virginity like that." I felt badly that our first time was a quick hard fuck against the wall. I'd never felt so out of control with lust before like I did with her.

"Like what?"

"Pressing you against the wall with my cock buried inside you. I should have been more romantic. Gentler with you."

She shakes her head. "I needed it that way," she says, disagreeing with me.

"But why?"

"Because all these weeks spent abstinent, I was starting to think there was something undesirable about me. I needed you to lose all control and take me like that," she admits softly.

"There is nothing undesirable about you," I assure her, bringing my hand to her face and rubbing my thumb along her lips.

"Show me…" she murmurs.

I reach down and stroke my cock that is hard again and lays extended against my belly. "This is what you do to me. You get me so hard and aching."

Her cheeks flush and she sinks her teeth into her plump lower lip.

"Think you can handle this again?" I ask.

Without exchanging a word, Sophie moves on top of me, straddling my hips and rubbing her wet pussy lips up and down my shaft.

Her confidence and sexual comfort level continues to surprise me. She knows what she wants and she isn't afraid to take it.

"Come here, sweetness. Take my cock."

She lifts herself up, positioning me at her opening and slowly begins to lower herself down. This time I enter her more easily, her silken heat enveloping me beautifully.

Unaccustomed to feeling so out of control, I bring my useless hands to her hips and settle them there, but allowing her to control the motion.

Watching her eyes as she takes me, something in my chest squeezes like it might explode. I'd never experienced a sense of trust so complete. It's overwhelming. She'd come back to me, believed in me to do the right thing and then gave herself to me fully.

"What do I do?" she asks, balancing above me.

"Ride it, baby. Take me deep."

She flattens her hands against my abs and wiggles

her ass, tossing me a sexy grin. "Like that?"

"Fuck yeah. Like that."

She giggles. "It doesn't hurt as bad this time."

I knew she was lying to me before about not being sore. When I'd washed her in the bath, the cloth I used between her legs came away with a tinge of pink, sending the primal side of me into a fit of rage. I hated knowing I'd hurt her, but I fucking marveled in the fact that I'd been the first man to penetrate her sweet pussy.

I frown. "You should have told me it hurt before."

"No way," she shakes her head, still concentrating above me on moving slowly up and down.

"Why no way?" I grunt. It's extremely fucking difficult to concentrate on our conversation with her tight heat strangling my cock.

"I wanted it, Colton. I wanted this and you right from the very beginning."

"Me too," I admit. "I'm glad we waited though."

"So am I," she says.

We hadn't even discussed protection this time, and the amount of trust that took between us felt incredible. Despite only knowing Sophie for a short time, we shared an intense, deep connection. One like I'd never felt before. We were both on the same page with not wanting anything between us. I was vaguely aware that I needed to be careful about coming inside of her, but my mind didn't work all that clearly where she was concerned.

Gazing down at me with burning blue eyes, Sophie takes me deeper and lets out a happy little sigh. "I love you, Colton."

As good as her snug body feels around me, it is nothing compared to the way its feels when she says those words. Love and acceptance and raw emotion rush over me. This isn't just a physical act. It is so much more than sex. Locking my eyes on hers, I rise from the mattress, until we're face to face. "I love you with everything that I am. I am yours, and you are mine, sweet Sophie."

"Yes," she murmurs, bringing her lips to mine.

I catch her hips in my hands and lift and lower her on me. "Fuck me beautiful girl. Ride my dick."

"Yes sir," she moans.

Sophie works her ass up and down on me – effectively silencing any more declarations between us. She feels fucking incredible.

Every time she rocks against me, I can feel her love burning right through me. White hot and so powerful it steals my breath. I'd never understood the sentiment *making love*, or how it differed from sex, but in this moment, I do. I completely fucking get it. It's a beautiful act. Two bodies sharing one perfect moment, racing together toward release. This is what I've been waiting for. This. Us. Face to face. Nothing between us but raw heat and sweet exploration.

Unable to lie quiet and still a moment longer, I lift

her from me and place her flat on her back against the bed. I move over the top of her and spread her legs wide.

"This time I want you to come on my cock." I push forward, sinking inside her with a swift thrust.

She whimpers softly and chews on her lip.

"Wrap your legs around me, baby," I tell her, pushing my cock into her just a little deeper.

Sophie moans, her legs lifting and wrapping them around my hips.

"Is this okay?" I ask, rocking forward again.

"More, Colton. Give me everything," she breathes, placing her lips against my neck.

Sinking deeper between her thighs, I thrust forward – hard - filling her with every inch I have to offer. I feel Sophie stiffen and I remind her once again to breath. She does, inhaling deeply and releasing a tortured cry.

I might be the one on top of her, filling her body with my cock, but I'm not stupid enough to believe I am the one in control. This girl fucking owns me. With her sweet nature, her strength, her innocence that she's letting me shatter and of course her warm, wet pussy. She's perfect. And she's finally mine. Nothing is going to change that.

Kneeling on the bed before her, I circle her clit with my thumb while I continue my long lazy thrusts into her. Her heat envelopes me in a tight, hot sheath, sucking my cock deep inside her. She's trembling all over, and knowing I'm getting close to the edge, I need to make sure she's taken care of before I go off. Our first time together, it was understandable that she didn't come with me, but this time I'm making certain she does. What kind of man would I be if I didn't make sure my girl was taken care of?

Sophie's low murmurs grow faster together and I know she's getting closer.

"That's it, baby. Let go."

Damp sweat trickles down my spine as fighting

off my orgasm becomes a physical ache.

I plunge inside her again and again, my jaw tightening. My heart is throbbing painfully in my chest and I'm about to come undone. I just need to get her there…

We move together, deeply, our eyes locked together. "I love you, Sophie."

She clenches around me, her body spasming wildly as she comes.

"Fuuck," I roar, burying myself in her perfection.

I wrap her in my arms and she clings to me. While we don't exchange a single word, the gesture speaks volumes. I don't even bother to pull out, happy to remain inside her for as long as possible.

I'm a controlled man in all things. In everything I do. From my company, to my charity, to stubbornly trying to manipulate the terms of my divorce, to buying Sophie that night… Yet all of that perfect order and control falls away in an instant. Love is unpredictable and uncontrollable. The force hits me like a thousand pound weight – weaving its way into every fiber of my being and taking up residence. I am deeply, madly in love with this woman. I feel like I've been cut in two, raw and vulnerable and unsure of myself for the first time in my life. It's terrifying, yet I wouldn't trade this feeling for anything in the world.

Chapter Nine

Sophie

"So sorry about the mess," Kylie says, ushering me inside her cute beach bungalow. "Thank God you're back though." She pulls me in for a one-armed hug.

She's frazzled – I can tell. If it wasn't for the crying baby she's bouncing on her hip, or the messy knot she's sporting on top of her head, the file folder she's holding in her teeth is a dead giveaway.

I pull the folder free. "Of course. What do you need me to help with first?" I ask.

It's clear she's overwhelmed, or maybe I just showed up at a bad time.

"Can you take Max?" she asks, handing me the crying baby.

"Sure." I grit my teeth. I'm no good with babies. Or animals. Or plants for that matter. I blame it on lack of experience. His screams quiet as he gazes at me thoughtfully, but it takes him all of three seconds to decide that he's not a fan. His cries rise to epic levels that leave my poor eardrums ringing. But Kylie has already disappeared into the kitchen, shouting something about needing to grab him a bottle.

Okay then.

As I peer down at the little guy in my arms, it occurs to me that I've never seen him aside from the numerous photographs Kylie has framed in her office. He's usually napping when I'm here, or with his nanny.

He's a chubby little thing with messy brown hair and giant bright blue eyes. And I would say he's adorable, but the ear-splitting howls he's letting out make it hard to judge accurately. I'm sure he'd be much cuter cooing at me and making sweet babbling noises.

186

I bounce him against my hip just as I saw Kylie doing, but it's no help.

Thankfully, she returns with his bottle and takes him from me. When the nipple reaches his mouth, he instantly quiets and the relief in Kylie is visible. Her posture relaxing and a slow smile uncurling on her lips as she gazes down at him.

"Okay, shall we go up to the office and I can tell you where I left off? I can finish feeding this monster and then get him down for his morning nap."

"Absolutely."

We head up the stairs to the office space above her garage that Colton so graciously had built for her so that she could work from home with her baby. I still don't know the story behind their relationship, and I make a mental note to ask him about it tonight.

Work keeps me busy all throughout the day and being back in Kylie's fiery presence – listening as she makes tough sales calls, doubling her efforts to secure more donations – makes me feel even better about my decision to return to LA. She cold calls potential investors and sells them on the project with ease. I'm sure she's heard about Colton's divorce settlement and the reduced funds he has to contribute.

Our work is occasionally interrupted by bouts of screaming that we can hear crackling on the baby monitor. Kylie works in fits and starts – darting from the room to retrieve a stranded pacifier, returning to the office to type a rushed email on her laptop, and later playing an intense game of peek-a-boo while fielding questions from an investor with her cell phone cradled between her shoulder and ear. She's truly a super woman. I never realized just how difficult it would be being a single mother until I see her in action. I'm exhausted just watching her.

When I arrive home from work, I know the motorcycle parked at the side of the house means Colton's beat me home. *Home.* I sigh, happily. Kicking off my shoes in the mudroom, I go off in search of him. I don't think I'll ever get used to how big this house is. Maybe someday I'll talk him into moving us into a cozy one-bedroom apartment. Though I'd miss the ocean views way too much.

I find Colton in his office, his tie loosened around his neck, white shirt sleeves pushed up his forearms and a crystal tumbler filled with bourbon. Hard liquor as soon as he's home from work? This is new.

"Everything okay?" I ask, sinking down into his lap and bringing my arms around his neck.

He sets down his glass and rests his chin on my shoulder. "Just work." He releases a heavy sigh. "Things are fucked up at the moment."

He doesn't normally talk about his work much, and I realize that I want to be let in to this facet of his life. He's the CEO of a company that I know very little about.

"What's going on with work?" I ask.

He lifts his head and meets my eyes. "It's nothing for you to worry about, sweetness."

I might not have an Ivy League education like him, but I was pretty sure I could understand whatever was troubling him. Maybe I could even help make it a little better. Isn't that what girlfriends do?

I rise from his lap and stand before him with my hands on my hips. "I don't think I have to remind you that withholding information got you into trouble before. You never talk about your work. Let me in. Let me be a true companion, Colton."

The frown line running across his forehead deepens as he watches me. "That's not…I'm not trying to keep anything from you."

"How do you know Kylie?" I blurt.

"Let's go have dinner and we'll talk about everything."

Oh, fuck. He has that look on his face like he has to tell me something unpleasant. *Has everyone seen my boyfriend's cock?* Work tomorrow with Kylie is going be extremely difficult if so. As much as I like and respect her, I will not be able to keep my cool if they shared some illicit past.

Colton

Once Sophie and I are seated at the dining room table with our plates of food in front of us, I know I can't stall any longer. I'm not used to bringing people in to my world so completely. Even when I was married, I rarely discussed my work with Stella. I don't think she even knew what I did, in all honesty. But I also knew it was time to change.

"First, I know Kylie from college. She and I were in the same business fraternity. And a few years ago, when I was founding my charity, I heard from a mutual friend that she'd moved out here and was looking for a job. I interviewed her over coffee. We hadn't spoken in a couple of years at that point. I found she was more than qualified. She'd left her job at a big marketing firm out east to enjoy

192

the California sunshine. I knew if I didn't snatch her up, she'd soon have multiple offers from bigger firms."

Sophie fiddles with her fork. "So there was never anything romantic between the two of you?"

"No." It's the absolute truth, and I've never been more grateful that I kept my dick in my pants than I am in this moment. I couldn't take another look of disappointment crossing my girl's features. "She's an employee, and that's all."

"Okay. Thank God, because work was going to be really strange if you two had some secret past." Sophie grins and takes a big bite of the food on her plate.

"Now, in regards to work. I'm not great at talking about my shortcomings."

She glances up at me and her expression sours.

"We had a bad quarter and the company stock is down fifteen percent."

"What does that mean?"

"It means that CNBC and various news outlets are discussing why the company is tanking and what the CEO is going to do about it."

"Oh. I'm sorry, Colton. I didn't know."

I nod. "I don't do failure well."

"This is not a failure, Colton. You are not a failure." Her bright blue gaze burns on mine. "You're a CEO at age twenty-eight. That's pretty freaking amazing. And what company doesn't have poor results from time to time?"

She's right. "True."

"Do you have a plan for how you're going to fix it?" she asks.

"I do." I'd met with my senior staff all afternoon to devise a six-month roadmap that would pull us out of the red. Hence why I was home early and hitting the hard liquor. It'd been a brutal day, but at least we had a plan. I'd been shouldering this burden alone, not wanting to worry

Sophie, but as she reaches across the table and takes my hand, weaving her fingers between mine, I see how wrong I'd been. Telling her – opening up this way – it hasn't made the situation worse – it's somehow made things better. It's at least put them into perspective. Work was work. It would always be there. There would be ups and downs. But this was my real life. This woman, who was taking me with all my flaws, and loving me anyway.

"You got this," she says, giving my hand a squeeze.

"Indeed." I squeeze back.

We continue eating, and then carry our dishes into the kitchen together. "I was worried for a second that your mood had something to do with Stella, or your divorce settlement," Sophie admits, rinsing the dishes and handing them to me one at a time to load into the dishwasher.

I shake my head. "No. All that's squared away."

"I can't believe just like that…it's all over."

"Yes, sweetness."

"Colton, I'm…"

"I know. I'm over the fucking moon about this too. Pace suggested I throw a party."

Her brow wrinkles in concentration. "We should do it."

"Seriously? You want to celebrate my divorce?"

She shakes her head. "No. I want to celebrate us together as a couple. We could invite my family, yours, get everyone together to co-mingle."

"I like that idea." I lean across the kitchen island and plant a kiss on her mouth. "What should we do?"

"I think the only appropriate thing would be a pool party."

"Oh yeah? I didn't think you'd ever want to go near the pool again."

"That's the point, Colton. It's time to move on and let go of the past."

My chest swells with pride. I love this girl.

"Come on, let's go upstairs." She takes my hand again. "I think a massage might relax you."

I raise an eyebrow at her. "You remember what happened the last time you tried to give me a massage?" The erotic images of us in the shower after her failed massage attempt are burned into my brain.

"I sure do." She smiles and pulls me from the kitchen.

Chapter Ten

Sophie

"This is so freaking weird," I say, turning to Becca.

"What is?" she replies, adjusting the ties of her bikini top.

"Dad is over there talking to Colton." *The man who purchased me at a sex auction, I mentally add.*

"So?"

Becca and I both turn and gaze across the pool to where Colton and our father are standing under the shade of the cedar gazebo, sipping cocktails and talking casually.

"It's just weird," I admonish.

She shrugs at my discomfort. "We're big girls, Soph. Dad doesn't care if you're sleeping with a millionaire. Shit, he's probably proud. I know I am." She grins at me.

I roll my eyes, thankful for the cover of my sunglasses. She's crazy. The anxiety I felt planning this party was mostly over how my dad and Colton would get along. I've never introduced my parents to a man before. Especially not one who's seven years older, runs a company, and has his own mansion in Malibu. It's little nerve wracking.

My mom has made herself busy helping out in the kitchen, clearly uncomfortable letting the hired help wait on us hand and foot, even though Colton and I both told her numerous times to enjoy and relax. I don't think my mother knows how to relax. It's something I'm just now learning how to do myself.

The day is pretty perfect though. The sun is shining brightly overhead. The temperature is perfect. Soft reggae music hums lazily in the background through the outdoor speakers and the bar is stocked with tropical drinks and icy bottles of beer. No one's in the pool yet, but brightly colored balls bob on the surface of the water enticingly. After much more laying out, I'm sure I'll be ready to take a dip myself.

Collins and Pace are seated at the bar, each with a drink in hand. It's early still and Beth, Colton's personal chef, has everything prepped for a barbecue later. Which makes me even more curious about what my mother could be helping with inside. She's probably driving Beth insane.

I take another sip of my mango daiquiri and try to relax.

Marta comes strolling through the patio doors like she's working a runway catwalk. For some reason the sight of her in her little red string-bikini makes my stomach knot. I hate that she and Colton had a fling – no matter how brief.

"Who the hell's that?" Becca asks, lowering her shades.

"Marta. She works for Colton as his personal assistant."

"She's gorgeous," Becca says.

Apparently Marta didn't quite get the casual pool party theme, her makeup is expertly done and she's styled her hair in perfect waves that fall down her shoulders and back. My own hair is tossed into a messy ponytail and the only thing decorating my skin is a thick layer of greasy sunscreen. I feel the need to march upstairs, add mascara and lipstick and change into my pushup bra-bikini top. Instead I chug down the remainder of my drink.

"Refill?" Becca asks, chuckling at me.

"Yes, please."

Becca waltzes over to the bar, introduces herself to Marta and makes brief small talk with Pace and Collins, refills each of our daiquiri glasses, then stops to talk to Dad and Colton.

She finally returns with our semi-melted drinks in

hand. "What was all that about?" I ask, accepting the drink and slurping down an icy mouthful.

"Okay, first off. Colton's brothers are hot as shit."

I nod. *Duh.*

"I still think Pace and I could have had fun in Italy…" she says to no one in particular. "Second, don't worry about Dad and Colton. They're talking about Colton's charity work in Africa and Dad is practically drooling, hanging on his every word. I'm pretty sure Dad's got a mancrush on your boyfriend."

"Thanks, Becs." I wondered what she was doing. Then again, spying for me was practically in the twin handbook.

"Third, Marta is nobody you need to be concerned with. Her tits are obviously fake and seriously, who wears heels to a pool party?"

I hadn't noticed her footwear, but Becca's right, her sandals have a four-inch heel. *Son of a…*

"She's trying too hard, Soph," Becca continues. "You're naturally beautiful and men prefer that over fake any day. Trust me."

I release a heavy sigh. I know she's right. Colton doesn't look at Marta the way he does at me. "She and Colton had a fling," I admit to Becca. "When he first separated from his ex-wife. I'm pretty sure she's not only seen my man's package, but she's had the pleasure of being on her knees before him, taking him deep into her throat."

"What a royal bitch."

I laugh, loving Becca's instant hatred for Marta.

"Seriously, sis, are you good with her working for him, given their past? If not, you should talk to him." The frown that tugs down her mouth is familiar to me. It's the same one I see whenever I look into the mirror.

"He had a talk with her. Told her that if she caused any problems between us, she'd be fired."

"Yes, but when she shows up here looking like

that, something tells me you should have your own little talk with her. A nicely phrased, *back up off my man, bitch*, ought to do the trick."

"You think?" I'd never imagined saying anything to Marta directly, but now that Becca is suggesting it, the idea fills me with both anxiety and a strange tinge of excitement. I've never laid claim to a man before.

I suck down the rest of my drink until the straw makes a loud slurping noise against the bottom of the cup. "Hold this." I hand it to Becca. Without giving myself the opportunity to chicken out, I rise from the chair and strut over to where Marta is talking to Pace and Collins beside the bar.

"Can I have a word, Marta?"

"Sure." She smiles at me sweetly and sets down her glass of white wine.

I lead her to the nearby set of cushioned chairs out of earshot of anyone else.

"So how is the redecorating going in the pool house?" I ask.

Shit. I can feel myself chickening out. This is made all the more awkward by the fact that she and I are kind of friends. She's been kind to me. She's taken me shopping and stayed with me when Colton was out of town on business. Of course, it occurs to me that all that friendship stuff could have been an act to get closer to Colton by befriending me. It's just not in my nature to be mean and it turns out I don't have the first clue about how to start.

"It's on track. I emailed Colton a link to a set of designs that I like for the space, but ultimately it's up to him."

I'm left tongue-tied and unsure of what to say next. I think we both know I didn't pull her away from the fun to have a private conversation about the new drapes for the seldom used pool house.

"Is everything okay, Sophie?"

"No. Actually it's not." I clear my throat, wishing I'd downed a third daiquiri before attempting this awkward conversation. "Colton told me about your past with him."

"Oh." She looks down at the stone patio between her pedicured feet.

"And while he assured me that he doesn't have any interest in you, I needed to hear you say the same thing." I pause, watching her eyes and focus on breathing calmly. She doesn't need to know that my heart is beating like a drum.

"At one time, I liked Colton. He's a smart, charming man. What woman wouldn't fall for him? But over the years, I've accepted that he doesn't view me that way, Sophie. I can promise you I'm over it."

I nod, still watching her, and unsure of what to say next. Geez, this is awkward. I should have made Becca come over here and have this conversation. Too bad we weren't really identical and couldn't pass for each other

206

because otherwise, I totally would have.

Marta leans closer. "Listen, the truth is, I know I can't compete with you. You're a gorgeous girl. And Colton loves you. If he hasn't told you yet, I'm sure he will, because I can see it whenever he looks at you…"

"He's told me," I admit.

"Oh. Well, like I said, I'm not surprised." She takes a minute, looking down at her polished toes again, before meeting my eyes. "I hope my working for him doesn't bother you. If it does, I understand, but I love my job, and…"

I hold up a hand, stopping her. "It doesn't bother me. I trust Colton. I just needed you to know he's mine now."

"I know," she says quietly. "I know."

I straighten my shoulders, my confidence rising. "Good. I am glad we had this chat. I'm fine with you continuing to work for him, but just know that I won't tolerate you flirting with what is mine."

"I got it, Sophie," she says, her chin tipped down, as if some of her poise has disappeared.

I walk away from our conversation feeling slightly odd and a little sad. When I relay the specifics to Becca after sinking back down into my lounge chair, she waves me off.

"Do not feel bad. Listen, Marta is flipping gorgeous. She's a ten. She will have no problem finding a man now that she knows it's time to let Colton go. You did the right thing talking to her. Now everything's out in the open and there are no secrets. Plus now that you're dating a man as utterly attractive as Colton, you better get used to beating the girls off him. That was a good warm up."

I nod in agreement. "Okay, good point." How my sister got so wise, I have no clue.

"I'm happy for you, Soph," she says. "Like really

fucking ridiculously happy. No matter what happens, I want you to live every day to its fullest. Laugh. Sing in the shower. Dance naked. Have sex with your man in the kitchen. Have lots of babies."

I gaze over at her, my stomach suddenly tightening into a knot. "What are you talking about? Why are you saying all this?"

She shrugs. "We just never know how much time we have left, that's all."

This conversation in the bright sunlight with Bob Marley singing *Everything's Gonna Be Alright* in the background feels totally wrong and out of place. I hate it.

I swallow down the lump in my throat. "You're healthy, right?"

She nods. "All I'm saying is that if cancer's taught me anything, it's to live every day like it's your last."

"Jeez. Don't scare me like that, Becca. We both have plenty of time for babies and everything."

"Of course. It's just that you've been focused on me for so long, now that I'm healthy it's time for you to focus on you."

"I've never minded a single second of being there for you. I would do anything for you."

"I know that. I just don't want you to have to sacrifice anymore." She smiles weakly.

I hate that she's right. I'm ashamed to admit that there've been times in my life that I resented her. Prom our senior year of high school was the perfect example. I had bought the most beautiful long silver strapless dress and was supposed to go with the captain of our high school's basketball team, Johnny Knight. Instead Becca took a turn for the worse and our entire family flew to Houston for an emergency surgery. I feel so selfish for even thinking it. I finally threw that silver dress away last year. The tags were still on it. And the guilt didn't end there. Now I felt bad that I hadn't donated it, but in a fit of anger, I'd stuffed it into the trash can instead.

"It's just that you've lived in the shadow of me and my illness for so long. This is your time now and I don't want anything to get in the way of that."

"When's your next doctor's visit?" I ask, changing the topic away from my own love life.

"I go in on Monday. But I'm feeling fine." She notices my now sour mood and her smile turns into a frown. "Hey, I'm sorry to get so heavy on you. I just want to know that no matter what happens, you're going to be okay."

"Of course I am." My life is coming together and Becca is finally getting well. We all have a lot to look forward to.

I lay staring straight up at the sun. Our conversation has left me slightly on edge. Actually the entire day has. Between my parents meeting Colton for the first time, my conversation with Marta and now this strange discussion with Becca…I've lost my zen sense of calm. *Poof.* It's gone.

My gaze strays to Colton and I see that he's watching me from across the pool. He's holding his cell phone in his hand and glances at my beach tote beside my chair and then back at me again. I fish my own cell phone from the bag, wondering if that's what he's signaling me to do.

As soon as I pull my phone out, I see a text from him.

You look stressed out.

I gaze up at him, wondering how he can read me so well, how he can possibly be so tuned in to *me* when he's entertaining guests. I love him even more in that moment. I type out my reply.

I'm not. Not really.

You're lying.

I glance up at him and smile. I love that he knows

me so well.

I'm fine. I promise. ;)

I keep my eyes on the screen, waiting for his reply
to come, but when it doesn't I look up at him again. He's
standing across the pool and I'm struck by the beauty of
our idyllic surrounding. There is nothing but blue sky
overhead, and the brilliant sun shining down on him
makes him look like a bronzed statute of a Greek god. His
bare chest and mansion of a home rising up behind him,
with only the expanse of sparkling blue water separating us
remind me how lucky I am.

Finally he texts me back.

Well I'm not.

What's wrong?

I want to fuck you.

;)

"I'm gonna go for a swim," Becca says.

Shit, I'm so wrapped up in my naughty text

conversation with Colton that I'd forgotten she was beside me. "Okay. Have fun." I watch as she saunters away toward the pool, and see Pace looking longingly after her, but not making a move. I briefly wonder if Colton's warned him to stay away from her.

Once Becca's in the water, I glance back down at my phone.

My cock misses you. I told him we'd have you later, but he's pretty fucking adamant it needs to be now.

Now? As in NOW?

Is he insane? We can't possibly. Just as my head is spinning, my phone chimes in my hand.

Yes.

I glance up at him and watch him type out another message.

Meet me in the pool house.

My nipples harden against my bikini top and my heart trips over itself in its fight to pick up speed. Without waiting for me to respond, Colton tucks his phone into the pocket of his board shorts. He says something to my father, who nods once, and then he strolls casually toward the pool house.

My own walk to the pool house is not so casual. I feel as guilty as a criminal on death row, certain that everyone is watching me and knows exactly what I'm headed off to do. My cheeks are already flaming bright red and my breathing is coming too fast. Apparently I suck at secret sex rendezvous.

When I reach the door to the pool house – that to any normal person would be a generously sized home – Colton is standing at the door waiting for me with an expectant smile.

"You came."

"Did you really think I'd turn you down?" I ask.

"No."

Taking my hand, he pulls me inside and shuts and

locks the door behind us. The three bedroom – two bath home is under construction. The wallpaper has been stripped from the walls and there are tarps covering the floors. Dust and random tools are scattered about.

All the silly little things I was worried about earlier fade away as I focus entirely on my man and this beautiful moment.

Taking my wrists in his hands, he brings each to his mouth, kissing the underside of each one. His smirk tells me he can feel the way my pulse is rioting at his touch. He guides me into the kitchen and stops us beside the stone counter top.

"Hands on the counter," he whispers low near my ear, his lips tickling the sensitive skin at my neck.

I swallow and comply, turning around placing my palms flat on the counter.

He moves behind me and I feel him slowly untie the string at my back. His hands move under the cups of my bikini top and he massages my breasts, plucking my hard nipples until I gasp out at the sensation.

Sweeping my ponytail out of the way, he tugs at the string behind my neck and removes my top completely, setting it onto the counter beside my outstretched hands. He kisses all along the back of my neck and my spine while his hands continuing rubbing my breasts and nipples. I push my ass back against him and am greeted by his thick erection, that I'm sure is barely contained by his board shorts. He releases a sharp grunt.

Colton's hands skim down my sides and push into the back of my bikini bottoms. He cups my ass, kneading it in his hands and then continues pushing my bottoms down until they pool around my ankles.

"Spread your legs," he breathes against my ear.

I tremble all over, but widen my stance, readying my body for him.

I hear him unlace his swim shorts, the crinkle of

217

fabric is the most delicious sound, as he pushes them down his hips.

"I'm going to feed you my cock. One inch at a time. Stay nice and quiet, okay?"

I nod and feel him begin to rub the head of his cock against me, testing my wetness.

Colton presses forward, just the broad tip of him entering me. I whimper and turn my bottom up, needing to feel him push deeper.

He retreats back. "You have to stay quiet, sweetness. We wouldn't want anyone to know I was fucking you in here, would we?"

I nod again. "I'll be quiet. I promise." *Just keep fucking me.*

One hand remains anchored to my hip and the other comes around to my front. He reaches between my legs and uses his fingers to rub my slick clit in tiny circles.

Pleasure rocks through me as an unexpected

orgasm slams into me. I pump my hips back into his, taking him deeper with each thrust.

"Colton…" I moan, unable to keep quiet.

He stuffs my bikini top into my mouth, muffling my cries of pleasure. "Shh…" he reminds me, "I want to make you come again."

I whimper softly, biting down on the fabric that smells faintly of chlorine and sweat.

Taking both of my hips into his hands, he pulls me back against him each time he thrusts forward, slamming into me, making me cry out. "You look so fucking hot, baby. I want to fuck your ass so bad."

He presses one finger inside my ass and the sensation—while completely foreign—is like nothing else. Pleasure grips me from the inside out. It's fucking hot. His finger presses deeper and he releases a strangled groan.

"So. Fucking. Sexy," he growls.

His cock swells and I know he's close.

"I'm going to come all over your ass."

He continues pumping into me while dragging his finger in and out of my backside and soon I feel my insides trembling.

My climax bursts through me and my muffled screams fill the quiet room. Colton wraps one hand around my mouth and slams into me again and again, milking every last ounce of pleasure from my body.

Then he pulls his cock free and I feel warm semen spurting onto my ass and lower back as he empties himself, marking my skin.

Holy shit that was hot.

He plants a damp kiss to the back of my neck, and then bends down and slides my bikini bottoms back up my legs. I'm all wet and messy from both of our climaxes, but the house has been cleaned out–there's no paper towels or running water even.

"Colton?" I ask, wondering how I'm going to

clean myself up.

"You can use the outdoor shower." His easy smile and eyes, bright with desire, challenges me.

I don't know what game he's playing, but if I go outside like this, there's a chance people could see me. Yet there's no way I'm backing down. I'm feeling spunky and full of life after our mid-day sexual adventure.

"Not a problem, Mr. Drake." I smile sweetly and his mouth drops open.

I saunter out into the sunlight with him following closely behind me, hoping that none of our guests notice the semen marking my lower back and thighs.

Chapter Eleven

Colton

She pulls the chain above her, water cascading down from the rainfall shower head, drenching her from head to toe.

I get half-hard again watching her. Streams of water run down her body and her nipples harden from the cool water. I have to force myself to look away to try and tame my erection. I've hit it off with her parents nicely and I wouldn't want to undo all my good first impressions by getting an awkward boner while I ogle their daughter.

Sophie trains her gaze on me and her challenging smirk tells me she knows exactly what game she's playing. Bad little girl. She'll be spanked later for trying to rile me up like this.

I raise an eyebrow in question and Sophie shuts

off the spray of water and wraps a towel around herself,

covering up all of those beautiful assets.

A shriek pierces the otherwise peaceful setting and

all eyes dart over to the patio doors. Kylie is toting a

screaming baby on her hip and a beach bag overflowing

with diapers and baby toys in the other arm.

I cross the stone walkway and take the bag from

her shoulder – no way I'm offering to take a screaming

baby. A calm one, I might attempt, but not this thing. He's

taking lessons from a banshee, I'm sure of it. No other

possible explanation for how he'd be able to reach those

octaves, otherwise.

"Thanks. And sorry about Max," Kylie says,

accepting my help.

"Not a problem. Is everything…okay?" I ask,

lifting an eyebrow at the banshee, I mean baby, in

question.

"He's been like this for days. Cries nonstop. He's teething," she explains.

"Then let's get you a glass of wine. Anything I can get for the little guy?" I ask.

She shakes her head. "No, hopefully he'll quiet down. I'm so sorry, I don't want him to ruin the party."

"He's not, Kylie. Not at all. Come, please, relax." I lead her over to the bar, where Pace and Collins have been parked all afternoon.

Pace rises to his feet, assuming the role of bartender. "What can I get ya?"

"Pace, Collins, this is Kylie. She's the mastermind behind my charity organization."

Introductions are exchanged while Pace pours Kylie a white wine.

"Are you sure you don't want something stronger?" Collins asks, smiling at the still wailing baby in her arms.

"I'm pretty sure my eardrums burst two days ago."
She explains, for their benefit, that the little guy is teething.

"Let me take him," Pace offers, crossing around the bar and stopping before Kylie. "Do you mind?"

Her eyebrows shoot up her forehead in surprise. I'm just as shocked. Pace is a tomcat on the prowl, but even he's not stupid enough to try and seduce another of my employees- especially not one who's a single mother.

"You can try..." No sooner than the words are out of Kylie's mouth and the baby's in Pace's arms – his crying stops entirely. The sudden silence surprises us all and we stand there, staring at Pace holding a baby.

"Hey little man," Pace says, bouncing the baby with one arm.

The baby stares blankly at my goofy brother, his giant blue eyes blinking against the sunlight as he takes it all in.

The baby grabs Pace's sunglasses, pulls them from

his face and begins chewing on the end.

"I'm so sorry, he's got teething toys in here somewhere," Kylie says, rushing to dig through the giant bag at her feet.

"We're cool," Pace says, sauntering away with the little guy.

"What is he, the baby whisperer?" Collins jokes.

We all shrug and Kylie takes a giant sip of her wine, her eyes on Pace and her son.

Pace spends most of the afternoon with the baby, holding him, bouncing him on his knee, swimming with him in the pool... and Max remains quiet and content throughout the entire thing – his wide blue eyes pinned on the man holding him the entire time.

"Is he usually like this with babies?" Kylie finds me and asks.

"This is a first," I admit.

She chews on her lip and watches them splash

around in the shallow end of the pool. I have no idea what she's thinking and frankly, I don't want to know. Pace and Kylie would be a terrible idea.

Later we sit down to a perfect meal prepared by Beth, and Pace relinquishes his hold on the baby only long enough to eat, passing him over to Sophie so that Kylie can eat in peace. Pace may have been fine babysitting all afternoon, but nothing will stand in between him and the pile of ribs on his plate. It's just as well, he'd probably eat the baby's arm off by mistake.

The sight of Sophie with a baby in her arms does something strange to me. My heart flutters in my chest and I absently press my palm against it, trying to get it to beat normally once again. *What the hell?* Sophie's babbling something to him, something I can't quite make out, but her voice is whisper soft and sweet, unlike I've ever heard before. I decide that I like it. Quite a lot.

She sits down with him on her lap and feeds him

little bites of crackers that she's broken into tiny pieces. I never knew this could be so captivating, but for some damn reason, they have captured my absolute attention.

***

When Sophie and I crawl into bed that night, we're both suntanned and lethargic from the afternoon spent entertaining.

"I'm glad our families met," she says around a yawn.

"Me too."

"What did you and my dad talk about?"

I guess she noticed that I commandeered him all afternoon.

"Mostly we talked about my work. A little bit about my family. Nothing too exciting. Just small talk," I lie.

I won't tell Sophie, but I'd told her father that I'm madly in love with her. She's it for me. I asked for his blessing and told him I planned to spend the rest of my life loving her. He stood there with a serious expression as though he was sizing up not just me as a man, but also my intentions. After a tense moment, he smiled and shook my hand and then welcomed me into the family. Our mid-day fuck was actually a celebratory fuck, she just didn't know that.

"Let's get some sleep, baby." I tighten my arms around her, hoping to stop any further questions.

Chapter Twelve

Colton

The following Tuesday at work, I get a series of phone calls from Kylie, then Marta and then finally Beth. I let them all go to voicemail and wonder if all of the women in my life have suddenly gone crazy. I'm meeting with my senior staff today, having a strategy session about trying to turn around the third quarter before the earnings report comes out next month.

When my phone flashes again, I glance down at the screen. The text from Kylie causes me to drop the stack of reports I'm reviewing.

Colton, answer your damn phone! Where are you?!

At the office, what's up? I type out, annoyed.

You need to come get Sophie. Her sister passed away.

Staring at the words on the screen, I try and fail to comprehend their meaning. We'd just spent the weekend with Sophie's family. Becca was fine. She was thin and complained of being tired, but she'd been fine. No. This had to be some type of mistake.

Excusing myself from the boardroom, I tap out a text to Kylie, confirming that I was on my way. I call Marta on my cell while racing down the stairs. There's no time to wait for the elevator, not while my girl needs me.

"Colt, where have you been? I've been trying to…"

"I know. Kylie just told me."

"Oh God, Colton, it's horrible."

***

I drive like a rocket all the way to Kylie's. When I reach her house, I don't bother knocking, I charge my way

231

inside, my eyes seeking Sophie.

Instead I find Kylie in the front room, her expression distraught. "Thank God you're here."

"Where is she?" I bark.

Kylie points to the back of the house. I rush down the hall and find Sophie sitting at the kitchen table looking down at her hands, a now cold mug of tea sitting beside her along with a half dozen used tissues.

The room is silent and lifeless. I fucking hate it.

"Sweetness…" I murmur against the hum of the refrigerator.

Sophie's head lifts and her expression is one I've never seen her wear and one I hope to never see again as long as we live.

Her skin is pale, her mouth is drawn into a tight line, but her eyes are the worst. They are blank and unresponsive – two haunted pools of blue that, despite her silence, scream of pain and trauma so deep my stomach lurches as I fear she'll never be whole again. Becca wasn't just her sister, wasn't just her best friend. She was Sophie's twin. It's a loss that I can't even begin to understand.

"Come here, baby." I pull her into my arms and she rises easily, letting me pull her to my chest.

She buries her face in my throat and sobs.

I clutch her tighter, hating that she's in pain and I can't do a fucking thing about it. "I'm so sorry." The words feel hollow and so inadequate, I want to swallow them back down the second they leave my mouth. I want to ask what happened, but I know now is not the right time. So instead, I let her cry, holding her tightly against me and muffling the sounds of her crying with my suit jacket.

A few minutes later, her sobs quiet and I smooth her hair back away from her face. "Can I take you home?"

She nods and lets me take her hand and lead her out to the car while Kylie watches from the doorway with a sad, wistful look.

When we arrive home, I dismiss the household staff. Vacuuming and polishing crystal vases suddenly seems far less important. I lay Sophie down in my bed, where she curls into a little ball, hugging my pillow against her. I take her cell phone from her purse and call her father.

"Mr. Evans?" My voice breaks and he makes the sound of a muffled sob on the other end.

"Colton, how is she?"

"She's in bed right now. Hasn't spoken a word yet." I wish I had better news to report, but it's the reality of the situation. "I'll take care of her, sir."

"I know you will."

"What happened? Becca seemed fine when she was here…"

I learn that when Becca returned home Sunday, she complained of mild swelling and pain at the site of her port catheter. Within hours, a fever had spiked and they

234

rushed her to the ER. The doctors began antibiotics for an infection that was roaring, unchecked through her system. Within hours of being admitted to the hospital, she'd slipped into a coma as the aggressive infection took full advantage of her weakened immune system.

Her reduced health had contributed to the problem – and the deadly infection had a direct line of access to a vein in her chest, courtesy of the port installed to make her cancer treatments easier.

Her father has to stop twice to compose himself. I tell him it's okay – he doesn't have to continue, but each time, he takes a few minutes to get himself under control and carries on with the story. When he's through, I have no idea what to say. So I tell him we'll be there soon.

After ending the call, I call Marta, instructing her to ready the pilot and my plane and to make arrangements for me to be away from work for a while. It's the worst possible time, but disaster doesn't plan itself around your calendar, it just sweeps in and punches you in the face, demanding your attention. And right now, this situation has my full and undivided attention – and my first priority is Sophie.

***

A few hours later, we're aboard my jet and it's ascending smoothly into the night sky. I had to carry Sophie to the car and help her board the plane. She's weak and disoriented and that haunted empty look hasn't left her eyes once. Not while she laid in the bed staring at the ceiling, not when I explained that we were flying home tonight, and not now – while she watches the little lights twinkling ten thousand feet below us.

I've packed our bags, which in addition to toiletries and random articles of clothing, each include formal black attire suited for a funeral.

I lift the bottle of bourbon from its resting place at the center console and pour myself a measure. Glancing over at Sophie, I'm reminded of our first evening together —this plane, her somber mood for an entirely different reason. She'd been fighting to save her sister's life. My stomach tightens and I chug down a bitter sip of alcohol, needing its numbing effect now more than ever.

It's only once we're up in the air that Sophie speaks her first words to me.

"Can I have some of that?" she asks, nodding to the glass decanter sitting beside me.

"Of course." I'd offered her water, tea and tried to get her to eat, all of which she'd refused earlier. And while I knew the strong liquor wasn't the best thing for her empty stomach, I wouldn't deny her. Pouring a moderate amount in a glass, I hand it to her.

Her fingers brush mine and Sophie's eyes lift to meet my gaze.

"I love you," I tell her.

"I know. I love you too," she says, then she takes a big gulp of her drink and grimaces.

We don't talk about what will happen when we land. I've never seen her childhood home, but now isn't the time for nostalgia. I want to provide her comfort and take away every ounce of her pain. This is the most frustrating, fucked up situation I can imagine. I hate it. I want Becca back. I want my sweet, full of life Sophie back. I hate the thought that crosses my mind – without Becca's existence, does Sophie's own existence dim?

She drinks two big glasses of bourbon, which I let her have against my better judgment, and then falls asleep against my shoulder.

Tightening my arms around her, I watch her as she sleeps, and vow that whatever comes next, I will be there for her.

Chapter Thirteen

Sophie

I never thought I had to fear an infection. Cancer – the big, nasty C-word was my enemy – not some illness that crept in uninvited at the eleventh hour. It isn't fair. And I don't understand. She'd been doing so well.

I hate how empty and lifeless our shared bedroom feels. Yet I can't help myself from laying on Becca's bed since it's the only place in the house I can still feel her.

I can hear Colton and my dad downstairs somewhere talking quietly. I don't know what I'd do without him. He is my rock and my love for him has only quadrupled in the past two days.

My mom comes in when the sun begins its descent across the sky.

"Honey?" she taps on the open door and enters.

"Hi, Mom."

She sits down on the bed beside me. "As soon as we got to the emergency room, Becca asked one of the nurses for paper and a pen."

I wonder why she's telling me this, until she pulls a square of paper from her pocket and hands it to me. "Even though we assured her she'd be fine once they got the antibiotics into her system, she seemed to know something we didn't. She wrote this in a fury while they attached her to an IV drip and removed her port. Then she folded it up and told me to give it to you. I haven't read it."

I hold the paper in my hands. It's still warm from my mom's hand and I savor the image of a determined Becca in her one last rebellious act against the fucking sickness that took her.

"Can you leave me alone?" I ask my mother.

She nods and rises from the bed, giving me privacy for what is sure to be an emotional moment.

I unfold the paper and laugh at the drawing that jumps out at me from the bottom of the page. It's a poorly drawn penis with large balls and squiggly lines of hair jutting out from them. I smile for the first time in two days. Tears dart to my eyes and my love for her grows, if that's even possible. I haven't read a damn word of her letter, and my mood has already lifted. She knew I'd need this. She knows me too well.

Sophie,

Thank you for taking me to Rome. Holy shit those Italian guys were hot. Thank you for being my best friend, thank you for every sacrifice you made for me, big and small. Thank you for always giving me your pink Starbursts.

I blink down at the words, recalling the countless

241

packages of Starbursts I bought from hospital vending machines over the years. The pink were Becca's favorite, and even though they were mine too, I always forfeited them to her. Every single time. Without question. Without hesitation.

I love you without end. Don't you dare think for a second that that love is gone. Don't you dare mourn for me. Miss me. Every day, just as I will miss you. Then get on with living. Do it for me. Because I can't. I will be there in every starry night, in ever whisper of breeze against your skin when you jog, I'm in every package of Starbursts, smiling down at you when you eat the pink ones.

A single tear slips from my eye and I brush it away before continuing.

Whatever happens, please know that I am with you. ALWAYS. Go love that hot man of yours, you lucky girl, you.

You two are going to make some damn fine babies one day. And that makes me so happy.

At the bottom is the penis drawing and her name along with a heart. That's it. The whole letter. I read it twice more, then fold it neatly along the same creases and carry it across the room, tucking it into my purse for safe keeping.

My mom taps on the door and enters again. Her face is open and expectant. "Well? What did it say?"

I take my time, considering how to answer. "Everything."

She nods. "Good."

Crossing the room to sit beside me again, my mom reaches for my hand. "What are your plans after the funeral tomorrow?"

We're having a luncheon at the house after the funeral, but I know that's not what she means. I think

243

we're all wondering the same thing – how do we go on living in a world where my bright, lovely sister no longer exists?

"I figured I'd stick around here for as long as you needed me. Colton probably has to get back to work, but…"

She shakes her head, stopping me. "Your dad and I will be okay. We've known this is a possibility for a long time."

Was I the only one so blind that I didn't see what was going on, didn't understand the risks? Becca continued wasting away while everyone fed me lines that the experimental treatment I'd miraculously funded did nothing. That word resonates far deeper than I'd like. *Nothing.* It'd all been for nothing. The auction, selling myself, meeting Colton…

No. As soon as I think that last part, I know it's not true. I'd be lost without him right now.

My mom continues, "Dad and I have each other.

You don't need to stay here, Soph. You should go home with Colton. Becca was so happy you found him."

I pull in a deep breath and nod.

***

When we leave Northern California it feels so wrong driving away and knowing that my sister is in that cemetery. Part of my heart has been buried in the cold, hard earth. She doesn't belong there. But then I remember her letter. She isn't there. She is in every ray of sunshine that shines too bright, in the whisper of the wind against my skin as we board the plane. I know for certain that she is still with me. I see her in my mirrored reflection of the plane's window, in the stray thoughts that are too feisty to be entirely my own. I feel her presence in the squeeze of my heart and I feel whole again. Colton pulls me close and tells me he loves me, and I think maybe, just maybe I will have the strength to do this.

Chapter Fourteen

Colton

Against my better judgment, I returned to work. Sophie assured me that it was important that we both resume our normal schedules. But as one week turns into two and Sophie continues her descent into a woman I no longer recognize, I know I need to call in reinforcements.

There were a few days there that gave me hope she was getting better. She'd gone for a jog, had stopped by Kylie's to see the baby once, and had actually talked to the grief counselor I sent to the house. But as I arrive home from work tonight, my heart shatters at what I find.

Sophie is sitting on the balcony that extends from my office. The wind is whipping her hair wildly around her face and goosebumps cover her flesh. A storm is coming, but she seems oblivious to that fact.

Her skin is pale, and her expression hollow. She's merely a shell of the girl I fell in love with. Giant blue eyes are staring blankly at the ocean and she's taking huge sips of my bourbon straight from the bottle. And the way she no longer grimaces at the taste tells me that this is probably a regular occurrence. *Fuck.*

"Baby?" I ask, approaching her with caution.

Her head turns in my direction and she blinks several times. "I'm losing it, Colton."

I kneel down on the deck in front of her and cup her face in my hands. "Losing what, sweetness?"

"Everything. The sound of her voice. The way she smelled. How it felt when we were together…"

I sit there, speechless, holding her cheeks and watch her eyes fill with tears. *Fuck, Colton, think.*

She's completely fucking broken right now and I'm worried that the only one who'd know how to put her back together again is Becca, the sister she shared a womb with for nine months, the best friend she loved without question. I'm terrified that I'm not enough, that my love will never be enough.

"I have to pee," she says after several seconds, then rises unsteadily to her feet.

I walk her to the bathroom, helping to keep her stable. "How much bourbon did you have?" That shit is strong. Strong enough to knock me on my ass after one small glass.

"Not enough," she says, her feet twisting beneath her. I grab around her waist, keeping her face from smacking against the floor. *Dammit.*

When we reach the bathroom, I maneuver her into the room, pull her shorts and panties down to her ankles and then sit her down on the toilet. "I'll be right outside the door."

She nods and I close the door behind me.

I can hear the sound of her peeing and muttering something to herself. Something about pink Starbursts. *What the hell?*

Standing in the hall, I fish my cell phone from my pocket and dial Pace's number.

"I need your help."

"Sophie?" he asks.

"Yeah. She's drunk off her ass. Drank a whole bunch of that hundred-year old bourbon. I'm scared and I don't know what to do."

"That shit's strong. Has she eaten?" he asks.

"No, I doubt it. She mumbled something about pink Starbursts."

"I'm on it, bro. Just breathe. I'll be there soon."

Just as Pace makes it inside the house, the sky turns dark and a loud roar of thunder crashes in the distance. The rain will be here soon.

"Where is she?" he asks.

"The bedroom." I'd laid her down with a photobook from my last trip to Africa. It seemed that she could look at the photos of the small villages, the people, the children for hours on end.

"What do you want me to do?" he asks.

"We need macaroni and cheese."

"You should have told me, I could have picked some up." He holds up a plastic bag that is filled with at least a dozen packages of Starburst candy.

"No, we need to make it homemade."

"How do we do that?"

"I don't know. Google it, I suppose."

He nods and heads into the kitchen.

"Bring it up when it's ready," I tell him, then head for the stairs.

Sophie is snoring softly, but when I cross the bedroom, she lifts her head and blinks several times, her eyes unfocused. I'm glad she got some rest, however brief.

"How are you feeling?" I ask, sitting beside her on the bed.

"Groggy," she confirms, pushing the messy hair from her face.

"I thought I could run you a hot bath. It might help you relax."

She nods. "Okay."

At least she lets me take care of her. She doesn't fight me on that. If she did, I'd really feel helpless and out of control. As it is, I know my subtle gestures may not help much, but at least I can do something.

I turn on the hot water and watch the tub fill. After dumping in a generous amount of something in a purple jar called *Stress Fix*, I go gather Sophie.

She lets me carry her into the bathroom, undress her, then lower her down into the water.

"How is it?" I ask once she's settled.

"Nice," she says and treats me to a rare small

smile.

My heart leaps, God I've missed seeing her happy.

"Will you be okay for a few minutes? I'm going to get you some clothes."

She nods. "You're coming back, right?"

"Yes," I confirm.

Once I have a fresh change of clothes for her, I reenter the bathroom, set them on the counter, pull out the stool from the vanity and sit.

"Thanks for staying." She grins at me again.

"Of course I'm staying. Do you want me to wash your hair for you?"

She shakes her head. "I washed it earlier. I do still shower, you know."

"I know you do." I did not in fact know this.

"I'm not broken you know."

"I know you're not."

I wait on the stool, and check my work email on

my phone while Sophie lounges in the tub. She sinks down into the water and rests her head against the edge, her eyes closed and a blank look across her features. When she secures her hair in a messy knot at the top of her head, I can tell she's still drunk by her uncoordinated movements.

My stomach churns with worry. I try not to hover, try not to stare, and instead focus on responding to the dozens of unread mail messages, but it's hard. Thoughts of her consume my entire being.

When I hear movement in the water, I glance up. Sophie has risen, standing in the center of the tub with streams of soapy water cascading down her body. My eyes wander lazily from the tips of her full breasts down to her bare pussy and I feel my body take notice of hers. My cock throbs, swelling against my thigh. The fucking bastard has bad timing. But a naked Sophie is not something I can ignore, no matter how somber the situation.

I grab a towel as she steps out of the tub and onto

the bathmat. She lets me dry her from head to toe, seemingly oblivious to my semi-aroused state.

Sophie stands there, watching me with wide blue eyes. When I grab the pajamas from the bathroom counter, a small pout crosses her full lips.

Ignoring the urge to kiss the frown away, I hold out the pair of panties, and dutifully, Sophie raises one foot at a time and steps into them.

"How are you feeling?" I ask. My voice is too damn thick with arousal. I clear my throat.

"Better," she says, her own voice just a whisper.

"Good." I'm glad the bath helped, and I'm hoping the food Pace is preparing will make her good as new. "I don't want you drinking like that when I'm not home."

I lift her chin up so I can see her eyes.

"I know." She swallows. "It was just a bad day."

Shit. Now I feel like an asshole.

I stroke her cheek and press a tender kiss to her

lips. "You're allowed to have bad days. I just don't want to worry about you, okay?"

She nods and leans in for another kiss. "I miss you, Colton. I miss us."

"I'm right here, sweetness. I'm not going anywhere." I press my lips to hers and feel the exact second the kiss changes, turns hot and filled with a lusty promise of something more.

Sophie parts her lips and her tongue lightly probes my mouth. Instinctually, I open, my own tongue running lightly along hers. I know I shouldn't be doing this, but it's been too long since I've kissed her–really kissed her and I'm craving her warmth, and a sense of normalcy. She sucks my tongue into her mouth and I swallow down a rough groan of pleasure.

Pulling back just a fraction, I check her eyes. They are shining bright with desire, weakening my resolve. It doesn't help that she's bare chested and warm and standing mere inches from me. I'm inches from having her heavy full breasts in my hands and my mouth, my face between her creamy thighs. I take a step back, needing to put some distance between us. Only I didn't count on that providing Sophie a direct view of the erection tenting my slacks.

Her eyes zero in on the bulge and she licks her lips.

Goddamn.

Focus, Colton!

"Here, baby. Let's get you dressed." I grab the t-shirt and try to help her put it on.

She takes it from me and drops it to the floor. "No."

"No?"

She shakes her head, her eyes still eating me up. "I want you...I want you to fuck me."

A fresh round of blood pumps south, making my

dick throb. "No, not right now. Not tonight." She's not in the right frame of mind. I'd be taking advantage. I list out a thousand reasons in my head, fighting with myself as she watches me.

"Please?" she asks.

I shake my head. "No. Now please get dressed." Pace is due up here with her dinner any minute. I certainly don't want him getting an eyeful. Her gorgeous rack is reserved for me and me alone.

She reaches down and clasps her hand around my cock, giving him a light squeeze. "Fuck me, Colton. Make me feel better," she begs.

I remove her hand. "No way. You're drunk. I'm not fucking you."

Bringing her hands up, she cups her breasts, lifting them together and rubs her fingers over her nipples. She releases a shuddery whisper soft sigh as though the sensation is the most pleasurable thing she's felt in a long time.

I stand there, transfixed, watching her touch her breasts. She's so beautiful I want to throw her down on the bathroom floor and fuck her six ways from Sunday. But I won't. I have a little more restraint than that. I would certainly be beating my dick later with very image in my head, once she was tucked into bed, but she doesn't need to know that. She gives her nipples a little tug and rasps out a throaty groan. Then she drops her hands.

Thank God her little show is over. I couldn't take much more.

But then she pulls down the panties I've dressed her in and begins rubbing her fingers over her tight bundle of nerves. *Fuck*. She's so incredibly sexy and desperate…

The panties drop from her knees and slide to the floor. My gaze follows their movement and I realize it's the same pair of pale blue panties she wore to the auction. I feel all my resolve fall away. I scrub my hands over my face. *Fuck it.* I shouldn't, but we haven't made love in two weeks and I'm desperate to feel her around me.

"Sophie, are you sure you want this?" My hands unconsciously move to my erection and I adjust him.

She follows my movements and nods. "Yes. I need it."

"Undo me." I look down at my lap and Sophie brings her hands to my button, sliding it free and pulling down the zipper slowly. Her hands work into the front of my pants, pushing inside my boxers and she takes my cock into her palm, gripping it tightly and stroking. A drop of fluid leaks from the tip and she smears it around with her thumb, causing my knees to go weak.

In that moment, I fully give in. If she wants a distraction, if she needs to forget all of the pain and misery of the past several weeks, then who am I to deny her that?

I grip her wrists, pulling her hands free from my pants. "Slow down, baby." It feels too good, and I want us both to enjoy this. I won't last if she keeps pumping my dick like that.

She draws her lower lip into her mouth and pouts before meeting my eyes. But what she sees when she looks at my eyes tells her everything she needs to know. I'm going to take care of her. I'm going to make her come so hard she'll forget her own damn name.

I lift her by her waist, setting her down on the bathroom counter. I step between her thighs, widening them and she tugs at my shirt in a fight to get closer. She's fully naked and I'm still fully clothed.

"Your shirt," she breathes.

"Yes, sweetness?"

"Take it off. I need to feel your skin."

I comply, unbuttoning the top few buttons, then yanking my shirt off over my head.

She tugs me close, until the tips of her breasts brush my bare chest and we both shudder at the contact and the rush of endorphins it releases. It's been too damn long.

I bend and take one of her gorgeous breasts in my mouth, my tongue laving her left nipple, then her right. Sophie arches her back and pushes her hands into my hair, letting me devour her. I want to take my time, make sure she's ready for me, but each time we're together feels like an explosion of sexual energy and I'm unable to control myself. Something I'm not used to.

I move back to kissing her mouth, my tongue greedy and sucking at hers. Her hands wander back into my pants, enthusiastically rubbing my cock. I know this is going to be quicker than I want it to be, but maybe that's what she needs.

With our mouths fused together and her hands in my pants, I find her wet center and push my index and middle finger inside. She gasps into my mouth, momentarily stilling before continuing the onslaught she's launched against making me come too soon. My other hand plays with her breasts and nipples, and Sophie whimpers while enthusiastically pumping me in her hands.

"Baby, easy…" I take her hands again, stopping her and feeling like a fucking jackass.

She grins up at me, clearly proud of herself. God, it's good to see her smile. If this is all it takes to make her feel whole okay, then sign me up.

"I can't wait any longer," I admit.

She shoves my pants and boxers the rest of the way down my hips, allowing me to angle my cock against her. When I shove forward, disappearing inside her perfect pink opening, we let out a collective groan.

"Yes, fuck me. Harder," she begs.

I oblige, pounding into her relentlessly, my frame dominating her much smaller one.

Her eyes wander down to the place where we're joined and she watches me slide in and out of her. It's an erotic sight – watching her as she watches us. I can read every emotion and bit of pleasure slashed across her features. When I push deep, her breath hisses out in an exhale and when I retreat her eyes follow the path of my glistening shaft with a hungry look.

Sophie

We make love against the bathroom counter, our bodies moving frantically together. It's exactly what I need — desperate, hungry kisses, the granite counter hard and cool beneath me, gentle fingers whispering through my hair, soft kisses pressed to my temple. I'm grateful to feel something other than numb.

"Yes, fuck me. Harder," I beg, gripping his shoulders.

Colton slams against me, his thick cock sliding in and out in a punishing rhythm.

My gaze lowers from his and I look between us to the spot where we're joined. The sight is erotic and carnal, and my insides clench around him, teasing a low groan from his throat.

265

"You like that baby?" He surges forward again, burying himself to the hilt and my head drops back.

"Yess…" I groan. "Harder," I beg again.

He suddenly lifts me from the counter, scooping me up underneath my butt and carrying me toward the bedroom.

He dumps me down onto the mattress and gazes down at me. His hard cock is wet with my juices and his abs are clenched tight, but his face is completely composed and in control. "Get on your knees."

I obey, quickly scrambling onto my hands and knees. Perched on the bed completely naked and ready, I wait to see what he has in store for me. Colton grips behind my knees, tugging me backward until I'm positioned at the edge of the mattress. He runs his hands along my legs, my butt, then pushes against my upper back – his hand resting in between my shoulder blades until I lower my chest to the bed. Turning my head, I lay one cheek against the mattress and gaze up at him.

He's still calm and in control and it's utterly sexy.

"You want to be dominated and fucked hard?" he asks.

I nod my head, keeping my eyes trained on his.

His eyes go dark and my insides flip with anticipation.

He aligns himself against me and pushes forward. I love the way my body stretches around him and I push back, drawing him deeper inside.

With one hand secured around the back of my neck, the other palms my ass. I feel his thumb rubbing against my back opening and I shudder. With his cock still pumping into me, he pushes one finger into my ass.

"Goddamn, Sophie," he moans.

Every sensation, every rough whisper of breath lights up my entire body. I push my ass back, meeting his hard thrusts. He's pounding into me, probably bruising me, but I fucking love it.

"Is this what you need? You need me to be rough?" He leans over me and growls against the shell of my ear.

I whimper with delight, my insides screaming: *Yes, yes, yes!*

His hips crash into mine, rough cries of pleasure clawing their way up his throat after each brutal thrust.

The orgasm slams through me, robbing me of air and forcing a rough cry from my mouth. I shudder, my insides clamping down on him, deliciously, as I come apart.

Finally, air rushes into my lungs and I repeat his name over and over. I feel the moment his cock swells and his hot release pours into me.

After, Colton rolls me over to face him, then kisses my face – my eyelids, my cheeks, my forehead, telling me how much he loves me. Then he brings me a warm cloth, along with my clothes, and cleans me up.

I feel sated and calm as he dresses me and tucks me into bed. My limbs are tired and sore and between my legs aches in the most wonderful way.

The past several weeks has been endless cycles of wine poured early in the afternoon to help me get through the day, sleeping pills that knock me out at night, and tears that flow way too easily. The grief counselor Colton sent on his first day back to work didn't help. She could not possibly understand the depth of my relationship with my twin sister. The loss has been unimaginable. My only form of therapy has been jogging. Just as it had been in the days when Becca was sick. It calms me, tires my limbs and helps me cope, if only for a short time. But as I learned tonight, intimacy with the man I love trumps everything else. I feel better than I have in days.

A knock on the bedroom door captures our attention. I didn't know anyone was here.

"Colt?" I ask.

"Be right back."

He shoves his legs into a pair of sweatpants and then goes to answer the door.

Colton

"Everything okay in here?" Pace asks, peeking around me to look inside the room. "I heard screaming."

"Yeah, ignore that."

His expression hardens. "Don't tell me you're thinking with your cock at a time like this."

"Fuck no. My every waking thought is about *her* – taking care of *her* needs. Not my own, trust me."

"And she needed..." He raises his eyebrows.

"Fucking drop it," I bark.

"Fine. Food's ready," he says, rolling his eyes.

"Bring it in."

I've dressed Sophie in a pair of pajamas and she's sitting up against the headboard, her legs covered by the blankets when Pace comes in.

"Pace? I didn't know you were here." Her cheeks flush as she realizes that she had loud, intense sex while he was in the house. Sophie watches him move across the room while balancing a tray in his hands.

"He cooked for you while I was...taking care of you."

She shares a knowing smile with me before turning her attention back to Pace.

The room smells like sex and I'm hoping he doesn't notice. If he does, he doesn't say anything.

"What is it?" Sophie asks, beaming up at Pace.

"Coco said you like macaroni and cheese and pink Starbursts." He treats her to one of his crooked grins, using my childhood nickname that has stuck.

"Starbursts?" Her eyes whip over to mine.

Her reaction is unexpected. "Is that okay, sweetness?"

Pace lowers the tray to her lap. There's a bowl of

macaroni and cheese that doesn't look half bad, despite being prepared by my shockingly-able-to-cook-brother, and a glass candy dish filled with pink wrapped candies. He must have opened all the packages and removed only the pinks. Nice touch.

Tears well in Sophie's eyes and she looks from me to Pace, then back again. "How did you know?" she asks, a single tear leaking from the corner of her eye. She brushes it away with the back of her hand.

I shrug. "I just did." I don't want to embarrass her by explaining that I overheard her peeing and mumbling drunkenly about the candy.

"She really is still here, huh?" Sophie says to no one in particular as she unwraps one of the candies, and places it in her mouth. She closes her eyes and chews it slowly, releasing a little sigh of happiness.

Pace and I exchange a look and briefly wonder if she's totally lost it, but then Sophie encourages us to sit on the bed with her while she eats, and she relays the story about the candy she and her sister always shared and Becca's last words to her in her letter.

My chest tightens as I understand the depth of meaning behind this and the incredible bond these two shared, as well as the sacrifices Sophie made to make her sister happy. My girl is incredible in so many ways.

After a few bites of the macaroni, Sophie thanks Pace and tells us that she's sleepy. Pace takes the dishes away and after turning off the lights, I curl around her on the bed, clutching her tightly against me and hold her until her breaths turn slow and even and she falls asleep.

Chapter Fifteen

Sophie

Becca has been screaming at me all day. As I sit around sulking in my usual fashion, I swear I can feel her. I can practically *hear* her. She's telling me to get up off my ass and get on with things. And I hate her for it.

I've returned to working part time with Kylie. I've been jogging several times a week. Things are back to normal with me and Colton. He no longer withholds himself from me anymore. He gives himself to me freely, understanding that our shared intimacy helps me. But I'm still not *me* and through some strange twin connection thing, Becca is calling me out on it.

I jog up the stairs and pull the letter from the special box on top of the dresser that I keep it in. I re-read it twice, looking for clues. The penis drawing still makes me laugh.

Focus, Sophie.

The third time through the letter, I get it. Realization slaps me across the face. She doesn't want me just going through the motions of my life – working, jogging, making love with my boyfriend at night. She wants more from me. She wants more *for* me. At the pool party she challenged me to live each day like it was my last.

I sink down onto the bed with the letter in my hands.

Shit.

I want to yell at her, tell her that it's not that easy to do. The truth is I have no idea how to go about it. All my life I've lived to please others. I kept good grades and never gave my parents a reason to worry –they had one daughter with cancer – they didn't need any additional stress in their lives. I was a good sister, a good person.

Polite, well-mannered, everything I was supposed to be. Selling myself at the auction was the craziest thing I've ever done, and even that wasn't for me.

Dammit, Becca.

I have impossible conversations with myself all afternoon, trying to figure out what she wants from me. Sky-diving? Bungee-jumping? What?

And then it hits me.

She never wanted me to do something crazy just for the adrenalin rush. All she wanted was for me to be happy.

"I'm getting there," I say to the empty kitchen.

God, I feel like I'm losing it.

I check the clock. One more hour until Colt is home.

One hour to come up with something to do tonight to prove to myself that I can do this whole living life to the fullest thing.

Colton

On the drive home from work, my thoughts drift to Sophie.

I don't know how I was lucky enough to go home with Sophie that night, but over the course of the past several months, I've been thankful for that fact countless times. She saved me from a bitter and lonely existence. And now I'm taking care of her through the hardest part of her life. But I see her progress little by little each day.

I'm helping her to live again – and remind her often that it's what Becca would have wanted. I stop on my way home from work and pick up packages of Starbursts, hiding the pinks around the house for her to find – one set next to her morning coffee, one in her makeup drawer, another in her running shoe. The smile in her eyes when she finds them makes my chest tighten.

I see her strength every time she laces up her running shoes, every time she cooks for me, in every smile, in every laugh – I can feel her bravery. She's choosing to live.

Of course, some days are still hard. Some days her eyes are puffy from crying when I return home from work, and it breaks my heart. But little by little, I'm getting my sweet Sophie back.

But tonight is the best. Because there's a little rosy glow to her cheeks and her eyes are bright with mischief.

"What are you up to Miss Evans?" I ask her, after arriving home from work.

"Nothing. I just have plans for us after dinner, is all." She smiles sweetly and my chest tightens.

We share a meal of roast duck that Beth has prepared and I fill Sophie in on the details of my company's progress. Things have really turned around. It's nice having someone to share the ups and downs with. She's successfully broken down my walls and taught me what it means to fully share yourself with another. In the past, I would have kept all my business shortcomings bottled up. Now I know there's nothing I need to hide from her. She accepts me as I am. It's the most beautiful feeling in the world. With her, I feel whole.

We finish eating and I'm just about to ask her what she'd like to do tonight when my phone starts ringing. I turn it over and the name *Stella* is displayed across the screen.

"Why is Stella calling you?" Sophie scrunches her nose in disgust.

"Good fucking question."

"Answer it," she says.

Christ. Here we go. "Hello?"

"Hi Colton," she says.

"Why are you calling, Stella?" The annoyance in

my voice is unmistakable.

"I have a few things I wanted to say."

"Sophie's here with me. I'm putting you on speaker." I click the speaker-phone button without waiting for a response. I won't have her wondering what is being discussed between me and my ex-wife, and I won't deliberately hide anything from her.

Stella clears her throat and momentarily stalls. "I never meant to be the villain, Colton," she says softly. Sophie squints down at the phone in my hand as Stella continues. "I was young and foolish. I loved you–in my own way–but I realized quickly after we wed that it wasn't a forever kind of love. You worked long hours, you were building a company at such a young age and were so driven and singularly focused. I wasn't cut out to live my life in the shadows of your work. I felt neglected and as wrong as it was, I let myself get swept up in the attention of another man. I felt wanted and desired and those were things I'd been missing from you. You provided everything I could want materially—but you weren't emotionally available to me. And I'm not blaming you. We just didn't have that deep connection. Your work was your first priority."

"Why I are you telling me all this now?" I ask, fighting the urge to roll my eyes. I don't know what game she's playing, but if it's forgiveness she wants, she's barking up the wrong fucking tree. She cheated on me – slept with our gardener, then took half my damn money. Relationships take work – if she was unhappy in our marriage, she could have talked to me about it.

After a long pause, Stella continues. "My lawyer mentioned in passing that you were out of work due to a death in the family. I was curious, so I called Marta."

I had no idea she was still in contact with Marta. For some reason that pisses me off. My gaze flicks over to Sophie's and her eyes go wide.

282

"Yes, we lost Sophie's sister, Becca," I explain. I take hold of Sophie's hand and lace my fingers in between hers.

"I heard and I'm very sorry," Stella offers.

"Is there a reason that you called, Stella?" My patience is wearing thin.

"Yes. When I heard about your situation I guess it struck something in me. I wanted to call and apologize. I realized that after all this time, it was something I'd never officially done and while I know that a simple *I'm sorry* isn't going to undo everything, I do hope you'll accept it."

I suck in a deep inhale. "Sure, I'll accept it," I say. It doesn't mean everything was swept under the damn rug, but I'm not going to waste the energy fighting with Stella anymore. "Anything else?" I ask.

"Yes, actually. I wanted to tell you both that I've made a donation in Becca's name. Two million dollars to cancer research."

Wow. I'm actually speechless. I look to Sophie, who's eyes are filling with tears.

"Thank you, Stella. That was very kind of you," Sophie says, her voice shaky.

"You're welcome. I'm sorry again – about everything." Stella says.

In the strangest turn of events I could have ever imagined, Stella has made amends and emerged as the hero. Well, not quite, but that donation was pretty impressive.

Once I end the call, I turn to Sophie. "Well that was fucking weird," I say.

"It was nice."

"I suppose it was." I kiss the top of her head. "But one nice gesture doesn't mean I have to forgive her for cheating on me."

"You don't have to forgive her, but I guess in a way, I understand her a little bit more. Plus, selfishly, I'm awfully glad you two didn't work out."

"Me too. Because I have you now." Her eyes find mine and they tell me everything I need to know. "Now tell me more about what you had planned tonight."

"I'd rather show you." Her eyes light up with mischief and I know my sweetness is back.

Sophie

Practicing my most enticing walk, I sway my hips as I strut toward the shoreline. The moon provides just enough light to see by and Colton's low hiss tells me he's appreciating the view. A slow smile uncurls on my mouth. "Are you coming, Mr. Drake?"

"Fuck yes," he says. His footsteps grow closer and with a squeal, I take off down the beach, Colton giving chase behind me. In a quick glance behind me, I see him strip off his suit coat and toss it onto the sand. But I don't stop until I reach the surf.

Taking a deep, fortifying breath, I charge straight into the water, despite the freezing temperature. There's nothing like charging into the ocean fully clothed to make you feel reckless and spontaneous.

As soon as I hit the waves, I begin to understand what Becca has wanted for me all along. The crunch of sand in between my toes, the cold water rushing over my skin, and Colton's bright smile as he watches me fight my way into the surf makes everything crystal clear. I feel carefree. Alive. With a flash of clarity I get everything she's been trying to tell me. It feels so good and freeing that I almost cry. But instead, I laugh, a raw, primal sound bursting from my lips. God, I don't remember the last time I laughed. Actually laughed out loud. It feels fucking amazing.

Colton's gaze snaps to mine at the sound and a slow smile uncurls on his mouth. He can feel it too. I'm back. I've got this. I'm going to be okay. I'm not merely going to survive. I'm going to thrive. I'm going to ensure Becca doesn't go quietly. Her message will ring out loud and clear if I have anything to say about it.

A sense of euphoria washes over me and I throw

my arms out to my sides, turning in a circle and looking straight up at the dark sky as the cold water washes over me. Then I swim deeper, needing more of this feeling.

Colton chases after me until I'm chest deep. Goosebumps break out over my skin as the cool water envelopes me, my wet clothes clinging to my body. The water laps at his waist and we stand there, watching each other, breathing hard. The moon is covered by a haze of low clouds, painting the night sky in a dark, luminous hue.

Colton moves confidently toward me. He is so at ease with his body, so controlled in all that he does, it's hard not to feel small and feminine in his presence. His strong stature commands attention. And he has mine – full and undivided.

He's unbuttoned his dress shirt and I watch the waves lick against his toned belly and chest, wondering if he'd taste salty from the ocean spray if I decided to lean down and lick him like my brain is demanding I do. A current of sexual awareness buzzes between us.

He finds my hand beneath the water and tugs me closer.

I reach for him and wrap my legs around his waist, relishing the feel of his hot skin against mine. With my legs tangled around his hips, my center is angled at just the right spot to feel the stirrings of his erection.

"Hmm, and here I would have thought I excited you a bit more than that," I say, feeling cheeky.

"The water's a bit cold, sweetness. Give me a minute."

I shrug. "We'll see, Mr. Drake."

"Trust me, you won't be disappointed," he says, his tone sure and authoritative.

"Good. Because I was looking forward to exploring something more tonight."

"More?" He raises one brow, watching me expectantly.

"More," I confirm.

His lazy smile is back and his eyes latch on to mine. "What's gotten in to you tonight? Not that I'm complaining," he quickly adds.

"Life," I say. "I lost sight of it for a little bit there."

"Understandable." With one hand still resting under my bottom, he uses the other to cup my cheek and sweep the hair back from my face. "You're my everything. You know that, right?"

I nod, letting the deep feeling of his love cascade over me. I've been afraid to feel these last few weeks, but now I'm letting every emotion pour over me and it's overwhelming – but in the best possible way.

"I can't lose you, Sophie," he murmurs. I can see in his eyes that he's been scared, even if he never said it, my behavior has caused him worry.

"I'm here. I promise."

Like a perfect sign from above, it begins raining.

Completely pouring. Giant raindrops cascade down on us and turn the ocean into a tumultuous force, alive with its own brand of wild energy. It looks like a giant pot of boiling water.

I untangle myself from him and swim toward shore. "Come on!" I yell when I notice he's still standing where I left him, watching me curiously.

When I reach the beach my clothes are twisted and hanging heavily on my body and my wet hair whips wildly around my face.

I grab Colton's hand – it's freezing – and pull him along, jogging toward the house while the hot rain pelts us from above.

Once inside, I sprint up the stairs, racing away from Colton's freezing, grabby hands against a bubble of laughter that I can't contain.

Colton's low chuckle rumbles from behind me as he gives chase. The house has been devoid of laughter for

291

so long, the sound is like music. Beautiful and full of life.

As soon as I reach the bedroom I dive onto the bed. Needing to get warm, I roll myself up in the fluffy comforter like a burrito. In an attempt to not get the bed soaking wet, I whip off my clothes and only emerge from the covers to fling them off – dropping the articles onto the carpeting with a dull, wet thud.

Colton's laughter dies on his lips as his hot gaze slides over my curves, heating me up from the inside out. After making their way up my body, his eyes land on mine. "You're so fucking beautiful," he says.

Somehow I know that he's not talking about how I look on the outside, he's talking about what's on the inside. The life he can see burning brightly within me. And I feel beautiful, with his dark blue stare eating me up and the deep love and acceptance I feel radiating out from his gaze.

"Come here." He holds out his hand and I rise

onto my knees, crossing the bed until I'm kneeling before him. Colton swallows heavily and watches me while he undresses himself, shrugging off the wet shirt and letting his pants and boxers fall to the floor.

A flash of lightning lights up the sky as anticipation pulses through me. Everything about tonight feels different. And I like it.

When our skin presses together, we're cold and clammy and sticky from the salt water, but his skin feels amazing pressed against mine.

After a few sweet kisses, he leans forward and takes my breasts in his hands, lifting them to his mouth and alternating between each one with hot, wet kisses and flicks of his tongue.

Oh dear God.

I reach down and find him hard and ready. I tug him by his shoulders down on top of me, loving the weight of his body on mine. Without warning he angles himself against me and thrusts forward letting me adjust to every hard inch of him as he fills me slowly but completely.

We fuck slowly, our gazes locked as we move together. We're quiet and the mood is intense and I love everything about this moment.

Colton's eyes watch mine as he continues his lazy thrusts in and out of me.

"I want you to fuck my ass," I breathe, planting a kiss to his mouth.

His lips still, his entire body goes as tight as a wire, as if he's pausing to be sure he heard me correctly. Then he kisses me again, his tongue sliding against mine, and he withdraws.

"Are you sure, Sophie? We don't have to…"

"Yes, I'm sure." My voice is sure and steady.

Leaning across the bed, Colton opens the drawer of the bedside table and removes a small bottle of oil.

"Remember when I brought this home?" he asks.

I nod. It's the massage oil he used to massage me my second night here. "Of course."

"You thought it was lubricant." He smiles. "Lay down on your belly for me," he says.

Drizzling some of the fragrant oil over my back, he begins giving me a slow, sensual massage. Working his way down from my neck, to my shoulder blades, soon his hands are on the globes of my ass and he's kneading them in his palms. My body hums in anticipation of what is about to turn into an erotic massage. At least I hope it is.

Every time his fingers draw nearer to my center, I lift my hips, giving him an open invitation to touch me lower. But he doesn't. He takes his time, rubbing my lower back, my butt, until finally I feel him part my ass cheeks and glide his fingers between my legs, spreading some of the oil over my back opening. A rush of tingles skitter out from my core and my body, ever responsive to his slow,

295

tortuous touches, comes alive. His fingertip caresses my forbidden opening and I have no idea how or why, but his touches back there feel incredible. Erotic. Sinful. And so sexy.

"You have a perfect ass." His voice is low, rough and thick with arousal. It only makes me want him more.

A low growl emanates from his throat and without further prompting, he slides one finger, then two into me, stretching me, readying me. The sensations overwhelm me and I groan out loud.

After a few more thrusts, Colton withdraws from me completely and I'm about to protest the loss of him when I feel the blunt head of his cock at my back opening. *Oh God.* My entire body goes tense.

He leans over me and plants a wet kiss in between my shoulder blades in an attempt to relax me. Then I feel his hot breath against my hair. "I won't hurt you, I promise. Just breathe for me. And relax. I promise I'll make this feel good."

I hear the slick sounds of him coating his cock in lubricant and then he's right back against me, spreading my ass apart and pushing forward.

I squeeze my eyes closed and focus on breathing, and relaxing my body, just as he said to do.

"That's it, beautiful girl. Let me in." His voice is impossibly tight and my insides go molten at the sound of his command.

He presses forward and sinks inside me, my body screaming out at the intensity of the pleasure and pain of being stretched. He pauses while I take a few deep breaths and then begins easing in and out in a series of shallow thrusts.

The sensation is like nothing I expected. I feel impossibly full and taken in a way I've never experienced before. In that moment, I am his. Every part of me belongs to this man. He owns my ass. Literally and figuratively.

Using my body for his pleasure, Colton pumps into me, taking me and making me cry out in ecstasy.

Bringing one hand around, he finds my clit and rubs me until I am quaking and bucking beneath him. The sensations are too much, and I combust, white hot sparks flashing behind my eyelids as I come.

Colton isn't far behind me, thrusting twice more before withdrawing and erupting in a hot, sticky mess against my skin.

He pulls me against him and I can feel his heart pounding just as hard as mine. We're breathless and move languidly, as if in a dream.

After a warm shower, we collapse into bed together, our bond deeper than ever before. My trust in him, in us, has grown exponentially after all we've endured, all we've shared. And I shudder to think what my life would be like right now if I hadn't met Colton. He is my life line. My savior. The reason I open my eyes and roll out of bed in the morning. He's my everything.

As much shame and guilt as I had for spending Becca's last months on this earth falling for and making love with this man, I know it was exactly as it was meant to be. My love for Becca will never be replaced, she will always hold the very center of my heart, but I know without my love for Colton, I wouldn't survive this. Her loss is staggering. And he pieces me back together again.

For that, I am incredibly grateful.

"Thank you for trusting me," he whispers against my neck, curling his big, warm body around mine and holding me tight.

His words are all wrong, I should be the one thanking him, but I understand just what he means. It took an incredible amount of trust to go home with him that night, to put my mouth on him that first time, to give him my heart, and now, to trust that he'll stitch me back together again when I need him the most.

"I love you," I tell him.

"I love you more, sweetness," he whispers.

Epilogue

Sophie

Six Months Later

"Keep your eyes off her tits, dude," Colton growls at Pace for the third time today.

I giggle and look over at Pace. He smiles at me not-so-innocently before fixing a pair of sunglasses over his eyes. "Sorry, Soph. I'm having quite a dry spell, and any time there's boobs in the vicinity my eyes automatically go to them, but I know it's no excuse," he says.

Colton looks ready to punch him. I settle my hand over Colton's in an attempt to calm him. "It's okay, Pace."

I look down at my bikini clad chest, making sure that everything's covered. It is. Thank God.

"Here, cover up, sweetness." Colton hands me a

beach towel.

"I'm not wearing a towel. I'm trying to get a tan," I tell him.

Colton bites his lip, stewing, but he lets it go.

We're spending a perfect day on Collins' yacht, and I have to admit, I feel like a bit of goddess. All three men have been very attentive, helping me board the boat, bringing me champagne, rubbing sunscreen onto my shoulders, and providing me with endless amusement as they bicker.

There are times I feel bad for smiling and laughing when she can't anymore. But then Colton weaves his fingers through mine and I know he's reading my thoughts. Becca would want me to be happy, so I push the dark, somber thoughts away and focus on the good in my life.

The sun is shining brightly overhead, making my diamond and sapphire engagement ring sparkle and glitter in the light. I hold out my hand, admiring it in the sun and Colton's answering smile is bright enough to light up a room.

The day he slipped it onto my finger was one the happiest of my life. I'd inadvertently found it in his sock drawer a few weeks before he proposed. I'd tucked it back away of course, but as the days passed without a proposal I'd started to panic, wondering if he'd changed his mind.

He hadn't.

A few days later, he flew us to Rome, back to the hotel I stayed at with Becca. And in the same hotel suite I'd shared with my sister, he proposed. We were surrounded by dozens of white flickering candles and big bunches of white peonies. After I said yes, he pulled a pink Starburst from his pocket and bit it in half, feeding us each a piece of it. It was incredibly sweet, romantic and heartfelt. Becca was there, silently cheering us on. I could almost imagine her grabbing my left hand, and making some obscene comment about how large the stone was.

The last year has been the hardest of my life, but I'd worked through all seven stages of grief. Denial. Pain. Anger. And now I've reached acceptance, though in my darkest hours, I never thought this day would come. Maybe I just never wanted it come. Never wanted to reach the place where I accepted her loss.

It's been a rocky healing process, but I've been stitched together by Colton's love and my own sheer determination to live life to the fullest. God had a plan all along. He knew he was going to call Becca home, and brought me to Colton in the most unlikely of places.

I know the ache will never go away, but I've begun to heal. To actually live again, rather than just going through the motions. And that the change in me is mostly due to this beautiful man lying beside me.

Colton is exactly what I need. He's smooth as silk when the situation calls for it, opening doors, pouring wine, helping fasten the pearl necklace at my throat. And rough around the edges when I need that too. His hungry mouth devouring every inch of me, a firm hand tossing me down onto the bed, pulling my panties down my legs and punishing my insides with his powerful strokes while whispering filthy words that make me blush. I love every side of this man. Crave them all. I thank my lucky stars that one man has been enough to satisfy all the different sides of me when I felt like I was splintering and breaking apart.

"We should have invited Kylie," Pace comments to no one in particular. The few times he'd seen her, he always regarded her with a mystified sort of interest. She'd been a good friend as I worked though my grief, bringing homemade soup over to the house and letting me miss as much work as I needed.

"She has a baby, she can't just take off boating at a moment's notice," Colton reminds him.

"I never thought about that," Pace says, looking thoughtful. "I could have watched the little guy…" he remarks under his breath.

Collins, Colton and I share a meaningful look, as if wondering what has gotten into him.

Becca's words from the pool party and her letter come rushing back to me about what pretty babies me and Colton are going to make, and I wonder if I can get him to sneak below deck with me. Who am I kidding, this is Colton. Of course he will.

"Hey hot stuff," I say to my handsome fiancé. "Do you want to go cool off below deck?"

His wicked grin tells me he knows exactly what's on my mind. "I love you so fucking much," he says. "Let's do it."

I rise, and tug him up. His full height towers above me, making me feel small. Then he laces his fingers in mine and I know I am going to be okay. *We* are going to be okay.

Our relationship has been unconventional. Unexpected. As he thumbs the ring on my left hand, I think to myself how we have come full circle.

"Can you believe we're here? That you will soon be my wife?" he asks, mirroring my thoughts. The word *wife* on his lips in relation to me sends little tingles skittering up my body.

"Who would have thought it would cost you a cool million to get a wife?" I ask, gazing up at him sweetly, but my tone daring.

"That is not funny Soph," he admonishes.

"What? I thought it was my incredible sense of humor that got your attention."

"No. It was your courage," he says, the conversation turning from playful to serious.

He gazes down at me adoringly and I can feel every bit of his love burning so intensely. I wonder if it will always be like this between us. Choosing to live in the moment, I give his hand a tug. "Come with me, sir. I need to give you a test drive before I decide how suitable a husband you'll make."

His mouth curves up in a lazy smile. "I will be the best damn husband in the world. Now get your sexy ass down those stairs before I spank you and fuck you right here in front of my brothers."

I turn and head obediently below deck, my body humming with all kinds of approval. I love all the sides to this man, but my favorite is when he lets his inner alpha male out to play. Today is going to be a very good day.

Filthy Beautiful Lust

Book 3 in the Filthy Beautiful Lies series

Pace Drake loves sex. He knows where get it, what to say, what to do, and he makes no apologies for satisfying his needs. But when he meets single mom, Kylie Sloan, he's enthralled by her, and begins to question his standard operating procedure. After all, there's no chase, no mystery when banging a woman in a nightclub bathroom. Kylie's depth and determination make the sloppy, drunken hookups that fill his weekends seem empty and shallow. She's the opposite of the desperate, clingy women he's used to. She doesn't want or need anyone to take care of her and that only makes him want to care for her more.

Kylie's trust in men has vanished. The last guy she was with played ding-dong-ditch-it with her uterus and left her with a baby to raise. Now her infant son is the only man she has time for, even if she misses sex and intimacy more than she'd ever admit. Opening her heart up to a younger man who's best known for no-strings-attached sex and his casual lifestyle is probably the worst idea she's ever had. But Pace wants to prove to her there are still a few good guys left, and watching the sweet way he interacts with her baby makes her want to try…but she can really trust that his days of hitting it and quitting it are in his past?

Acknowledgements

I have the best readers on the planet. Hands down. A tremendous thank you for making Filthy Beautiful Lies a New York Times & USA Today bestseller. Thank you for loving Colton and Sophie and getting just as wrapped up in their story as I did.

Danielle Sanchez, you are a little publicity goddess. Thank you for your organization and all of the planning and work that goes into launching a book. Whew. I'm tired just thinking about it. And incredibly grateful for you.

My lovely author friends who read my rough drafts, provide oh-so-helpful suggestions and cheer me on when I want to throw in the towel. Rachel Brookes, Meghan March, Emma Hart – you are all so wonderful.

Thank you to all the bloggers who have supported this series, posted reviews and told all their friends. My sincerest gratitude to you.

Last, to my two baby boys and darling husband....

You own my heart.

Tell Me Your Favorite Part!

If you enjoyed Filthy Beautiful Love, I invite you to head over to the retailer where you purchased it (Amazon, Barnes & Noble, iTunes, etc.) and let me know which part was your favorite. Reading reviews is often the highlight of my day, plus they help new readers discover the book. I thank you in advance!

Connect With Me At:

http://www.kendallryanbooks.com

http://www.facebook.com/kendallryanbooks

http://www.twitter.com/kendallryan1

Also By Kendall Ryan:

Unravel Me

Make Me Yours

Resisting Her

Hard to Love

Working It

Craving Him

All or Nothing

When I Break

When I Surrender

When We Fall

Printed in Great Britain
by Amazon.co.uk, Ltd.,
Marston Gate.